Miss Bianca

With Illustrations By
Garth Williams

By Margery Sharp

MISS
BIANCA

A Yearling Book

A YEARLING BOOK

Published by
Dell Publishing Co., Inc.
1 Dag Hammarskjold Plaza
New York, New York 10017

Yearling ® TM 913705, Dell Publishing Co., Inc.
ISBN: 0-440-45761-0

Reprinted by arrangement with Little, Brown and Company
Printed in the United States of America
Seventh Dell Printing—March 1980

MPC

Contents

Miss Bianca

1

The General Meeting

HOWEVER PERILOUS and astonishing the exploits of the Mouse Prisoners' Aid Society, each separate adventure always starts off at a formal General Meeting. (Corporate rules and regulations, order and decorum, provide a solid foundation for individual heroism.) On this particular occasion the chair was taken by none other than the celebrated Miss Bianca, whose part in rescuing a prisoner from the Black Castle earned her the first Nils and Miss Bianca Medal ever struck.

What a picture she made, as she stood modestly waiting on the platform for the applause to subside! — her coat ermine-white, her long dark lashes fluttering over her huge brown eyes — round her neck a very fine silver chain — her whole tiny, exquisite figure thrown into graceful relief against a background of potted palms! But beneath that composed exterior her heart was in fact beating like a very small

3

sledge hammer, for Miss Bianca had been drawn into public life against her will; the elegant retreat of a Porcelain Pagoda, in the schoolroom of an Ambassador's son, was far more agreeable to her than the agitation of a Moot-hall. Fortunately the handsome building, converted from an empty wine cask, still retained the aroma of a notable claret; it acted on Miss Bianca's nostrils like a sort of sal volatile. Even so, her famous silvery voice, when she was at last able to speak, slightly trembled.

"And now," said Miss Bianca, consulting her notes, "we come to the main item on the Agenda. It is really the Secretary's place to put it to you —"

"No, no!" cried all the mice at once. (At least a hundred; the Ladies' Guild was out in force, every matchbox bench was filled, there was standing at the back.) "No, no! Miss Bianca!"

Miss Bianca glanced apologetically over her shoulder; the Secretary smiled, and shook his head. He was a rather commonplace-looking mouse named Bernard: though he too had adventured to the Black Castle no one ever seemed to remember it, and he would probably have been made Secretary anyway, just because he was so reliable about mailing notices.

"Very well, then," said Miss Bianca. "Can everyone hear me at the back?"

4

"Aye, aye!" "Clear as a bell!" "Even Granddad!" called several of the standees.

"Then I will proceed," said Miss Bianca. "What I am about to say will no doubt surprise you, but I rely as always upon your open minds and generous hearts." (Miss Bianca might be a nervous speaker, but she was by this time also a practiced one, and knew there was nothing like flattery to win an audience to one's side. Moreover, people *told* they are generous and open-minded often discover that they really *are,* so that flattery of the right kind — and Miss Bianca would have scorned to employ any other — does nothing but good.) "In the past," continued Miss Bianca, "as you are well aware, our Society has directed its efforts along the traditional lines of cheering, consoling, and generally befriending the prisoner in his cell —"

"One of 'em us even got out!" cried an excited young mouse. "And from the Black Castle! If it's a rescue operation again, ma'am, count on me!"

"And me!" "And me!" shouted two more, jumping to their feet and flexing their biceps. For a moment there was quite a turmoil as their mothers tried to make them sit down and their friends slapped them on the back; it was such a scene of excitement and disorder as the Moot-hall rarely witnessed. — Miss

Bianca, however, again glanced anxiously at the Secretary, and he knew exactly what she was thinking: that their common adventure had given mice an unfortunate taste for *flamboyance* in welfare work. Not one, now, thought anything of sitting up to beg a prisoner's crumb! — in the long run one of the most useful acts a mouse can perform. Crumb-begging, like waltzing in circles (even with a jailer outside the door), was regarded as mere National Service stuff, barely worth reporting on one's return from the regulation three weeks' duty . . .

"Only tell us, ma'am, what chap it is we're to rescue *this* time!" one of the would-be heroes was shouting. "A soldier taken in the cruel wars?"

"Or a brave mariner taken by pirates?" shouted his friend. "Oh what joy to nibble at the halyard, till the Jolly Roger hits the deck!"

Miss Bianca cut them both short.

"*This* time, it isn't a 'chap' at all," she said severely. "*This* time, it's a little girl."

2

As she had only too rightly anticipated, the excitement dwindled and dissipated like the air from a pricked balloon. Quite apart from the general feeling of let-down, mice have small use for little girls. Little girls are too fond of kittens. There was a sudden rumble in the Hall as the audience shifted in its seats — of matchbox jarring against matchbox, of voices lowered to be sure, but definitely grumbling-ish. Miss Bianca saw that she must employ all her eloquence. She did. Dropping all note of severity, and just as sweetly and blandly as if the grumbling had been applause —

"The child's name," she proceeded, "is Patience. A pretty one, is it not? — reminding us also of that virtue which I'm sure every mother present, especially those with bold sons, needs to employ twenty times a day! *Patience* has no mother, however, nor father, nor indeed any relative in the world; and she is only eight years old."

This touching exordium was not without effect. All mice have such large families themselves, and are so used to counting aunts and uncles by the score, and first cousins by the hundred, they can imagine nothing worse than having no relations at all. A motherly-looking member of the Ladies' Guild began to sniff at once.

"Poor little thing!" she sniffed. "Are her eyes open yet?"

"Only just wide enough," said Miss Bianca gravely,

"to appreciate the full horror of her situation. For horrible it is, as I am sure you will agree, when I tell you that this unfortunate innocent has been kidnapped into the service of the Grand Duchess!"

3

What a change, again, came over the Moot-hall! — instead of rumbling, utter quiet; instead of grumbling, the tense silence of bated breath! For even the stern rulers of the State feared the Grand Duchess — so old, and rich, and tyrannical, so withdrawn from all eyes within her Diamond Palace!

Humbler folk believed her to be a witch.

The three would-be heroes' mothers absolutely pulled them down by the tail. Not that they needed much pulling.

"So she's in the Diamond Palace, eh?" said a sour voice.

"Indeed she is," said Miss Bianca, more brightly than she felt. "Within the very center of our city! At least there will be no perilous journey to undertake first, as there was to the Black Castle! I don't suppose there's one of you here couldn't find your way to the Palace blindfolded."

"Aye, but not with our eyes open," objected the

voice. It belonged to a peculiarly disagreeable old
Professor of Mathematics, who made a point of ob-
jecting to everything, from barn dances to lending
libraries; in this case, however, he obviously had the
Meeting with him. Miss Bianca looked urgently
towards Bernard — it was just at such junctures as
these that the Secretary's stolid, matter-of-fact manner
was most valuable. He at once rose and stumped to
the platform's edge.

"Erected in 1775, and thus one of the country's
most historic monuments," began Bernard, just like

a guidebook, "of course the Diamond Palace isn't actually *built* of diamonds. It's built of rock crystal. That is, there's nothing magic about it. It's just an ordinary, rock-crystal palace."

"As I suppose the Duchess is just an ordinary Duchess?" sneered the Professor.

"Born in 1883," agreed Bernard, "only d. and sole issue of the late Grand Duke Tiberius, therefore inheriting all his titles and properties — the Diamond Palace among 'em, also a certain hunting lodge — "

"Never mind the hunting lodge," interrupted the Professor. "Does she ever open *bazaars?*"

"Not that I know of," admitted Bernard.

"Or flower shows?"

"Not that I've heard of," admitted Bernard.

"Then of course she isn't an ordinary Duchess," snapped the Professor. "In my opinion, she's a witch."

Undoubtedly he had the Meeting with him. Low mutterings of "Hear, hear!" rose from every side. This was particularly chagrining to Bernard, who had really done his best. — However, Miss Bianca, as she swiftly advanced again, threw him a very kind look. (Bernard noted it in his diary that night.)

"Such I know to be the common view," said Miss Bianca smoothly, "among the uneducated." (This was of course a dreadfully shrewd hit at a Professor of

Mathematics.) "To the educated view, the Grand Duchess is simply a cruel, cold-hearted, tyrannous old woman, which Heaven knows is bad enough! — Has anyone here read *Jane Eyre?*"

The question, however unexpected, was almost superfluous. Mice are great readers — as every librarian knows. A forest of hands shot up; quite a shudder ran through the Hall as half the assembly recalled poor Jane's various, unmerited hardships — such as being made to stand on a high stool, also nothing but burnt porridge for breakfast. Several members of the Ladies' Guild, in telepathic communication with each other and Miss Bianca, squeaked that it didn't ought to be allowed.

"I agree with you," said Miss Bianca gravely. "Yet what was the worst hardship of all? The deprivation of all affection. Not to be kissed good-night (at the tender age of eight) is a deprivation indeed."

At this point many of the mothers present kissed their offspring so to speak on principle, and just in case of accidents. It was amid a general wiping of whiskers that Miss Bianca launched her boldest stroke.

"To the imagination of the *male* members of our Society," she continued, with rising intensity, "it is perhaps impossible for me to appeal. How carelessly indeed each son takes for granted a mother's love! But surely the female breast, though so much more tender, is no less heroic? — I don't appeal to the *men*," cried Miss Bianca, "I appeal to the Ladies' Guild!"

4

Here was something new indeed!

Hitherto, the Ladies' Guild had never done anything more exciting than provide supper. Its members listened all the more eagerly. Many of them stood up on the benches — pushing their husbands off in the process!

"If the adventure be too doubtful for our menfolk," went on Miss Bianca, more sweetly and persuasively than ever, "may not we ladies undertake it? Of course I wouldn't ask you to attack pirates, or armed sentries — that would be *quite* beyond us: but the child Patience is under the surveillance only of ladies-in-waiting. Should you wish to hear my plan —"

"Yes, yes!" "Tell it quick!" cried all the Ladies' Guild.

"First, then, we infiltrate into the Diamond Palace. — As you have just heard the Secretary explain, it's a perfectly ordinary Palace," added Miss Bianca reassuringly, "and no more difficult to infiltrate than any other. — Next, being assembled, under my leadership — if you will accept of it —"

"Yes, yes!" cried the Ladies' Guild again.

"— at a given signal all rush squeaking forth. What will the ladies-in-waiting do *then?*"

Instantly the full beauty of the plan was apparent.

"Jump on chairs!" cried an excited voice.

"*Some* may," conceded Miss Bianca, "but for the most part they will *run*. Anywhere, in all directions — flinging open every door before them! Certainly not one will have a thought for the child! — who may thus, in the general confusion and panic, easily make her escape. It will not be a case of 'see how *we* run,' " cried Miss Bianca — referring to one of the oldest mouse legends of all, that of the Three Blind Mice — "but 'see how *they* run'!"

She sat down amid a positive hurricane of shrill cheers. One section of the Ladies' Guild tried to storm the platform, while other members gathered in excited groups discussing ways and means of infiltration. A tough games-mistress mouse offered to arrange training courses up chair rungs. They were all filled with pride and enthusiasm at the thought of doing something so daring and important, and such a wonderful change from just providing suppers.

It was not to be expected, however, that their husbands were going to take all this lying down. As the wives gathered in chattering knots, so did they (except that they rather muttered). Nor was it long before they found a spokesman. Miss Bianca had scarcely recovered from her exertions when up rose the Professor again.

"Just a minute," said he.

Miss Bianca sighed. But with her usual beautiful manners she with a graceful gesture of one hand silenced the Ladies' Guild (who were quite ready to shout him down), and with an equally graceful gesture of the other invited him to proceed.

"No one less than I," proceeded the Professor, "denigrates the heroic potentialities of the Ladies' Guild — particularly under the leadership of our esteemed Chairwoman. In fact, I consider the child Patience as rescued already. All I ask — and am maybe not alone in so asking —"

("Hear, hear!" muttered all the husbands.)

"— is what do we *do* with her when we've *got* her? Other prisoners — *proper* prisoners — have homes to go to. This child, on Madam Chairwoman's own admission, has no home at all."

"If she's not very big, I dare say she could come in with my lot behind the stove," suggested the motherly mouse. "One more in a dozen won't make much differ!"

"Don't forget she's going to *grow*," warned the Professor. "My word, what a size she'll be, in a month or two's time! Eating enough for a couple of hundred! — Is she to be on our hands for *generations?*"

Undoubtedly he scored a point. Mice have enough work to feed their own enormous families. Even the whiskers of the Ladies' Guild members began to droop, as they recalled what a struggle Sunday dinner sometimes was . . .

Loyal and devoted to Miss Bianca, and the Prisoners' Aid Society, as they wanted to be, their whiskers undeniably drooped.

Not for long!

"But of course all *that's* been arranged for," said Miss Bianca. "She will go to the Happy Valley . . ."

2

The Happy Valley

IN THE BIG comfortable kitchen of a farmhouse
in the Happy Valley a farmer and his wife were sitting
after supper. It was a lovely room. All the furniture
was beautifully polished, and the floor strewn with
fresh-cut sweet-smelling rushes: in the window sill a
row of geraniums splashed big scarlet blossoms against
the warm woollen curtain-stuff, colored pale green
with brown stripes. Two big lamps — one for the
wife's mending basket, the other for her husband's
newspaper — cast each a pool of soft amber light,
while up on the ceiling little lesser gleams, reflected
from the log fire, made ever-changing patterns as they
chased the shadows. Nothing could have been more
cosy and secure, or more pleasant and peaceful. —
But the woman sighed.

"What ails you, wife?" asked her husband kindly.
She tried her best to smile.

"Only foolishness, husband. 'Tis only that when the flames play so over the ceiling I remember our little lost one most. She called them — don't you remember? — the elves going to market."

"You've two great boys still," said the farmer.

"Which don't I well know and am thankful for," said his wife. "There's their supper waiting hot in the oven till they get home from their dancing — my big bad boys, handsome as their Dad, out breaking hearts right and left! But I still miss our little daughter."

"I no less," said the farmer, "bringing me my slippers . . ."

"So do the boys miss their merry little sister," said his wife. "What games they had together in the hay — and snowballing in winter, and cowslip-gathering in the spring!"

"Aye, and going after nuts in autumn," said the farmer.

"What care they took of her, too! I could trust her with them even paddling in the brook . . . Now there's the cowslips and the hazelnuts still, and two kind brothers still, but no little maid to find happiness in 'em."

"She was happiest of all on my knee," said the farmer sadly, "or in your lap, wife."

The little flames chased in and out among the

rafters as though they were looking for someone. As though at a breath of wind, or a sigh, one of the geraniums in the window gently let fall a scattering of scarlet petals.

"D'you know what I dreamed last night, husband?" said the woman softly. "Of a little girl-child coming to our door, to be taken in and cherished . . ."

"Such dreams are only dreams," said the farmer, "it's best not to think of them. — I've seen a mouse in the larder," he added, in a clumsy though well-meant effort to change the melancholy subject. "Give me a bit of bacon and I'll set a trap."

"Not in *my* larder you won't!" said his wife. " 'Let *nibble who needs*,' " she quoted, "I'm sure we've enough and to spare!"

2

Actually the mouse in the larder was Miss Bianca! Here it is necessary to go back a bit.

As soon as she heard of Patience's dreadful fate, Miss Bianca, who was as sensible as she was kind, not only determined upon a rescue but also looked ahead to the child's future, and at once circularized all the Country Members of the Prisoners' Aid Society for news of a suitable foster home. When a reply came in from the Happy Valley, she was delighted. It was the most beautiful part of the whole country — farmland so rich, gleaners left a whole winter supply (for a mouse) in each furrow; the cheeses and sausages and sides of bacon stored in the larders of its farmhouses, only the pen of a poet could describe. Nor were the fortunate inhabitants less generous than their soil; they were simply the kindest, best-hearted folk imaginable, and probably not a farmwife in the Valley would have refused to take Patience in — only this particular one, as has been seen, was particularly suitable.

Nonetheless, Miss Bianca investigated. Reliable as her correspondent had sounded, when it came to an enterprise of such moment she felt she must see things for herself; and unknown to Bernard took the occasion of a Diplomatic picnic to do so. The Ambassador's car, slowing down at an awkward turning by the farm-house gates (where a great oak tree took up half the road), more or less put her down at her destination; the Ambassador's son (who knew he shouldn't have had Miss Bianca in his pocket at all) raised no alarm; and off Miss Bianca ran to investigate.

She always did things thoroughly. Before entering the house at all, first she looked into the cow byre —

all sweet and wholesome, warm with the breath of clean contented cows. ("Pray pardon the intrusion," said Miss Bianca. "None needed, none needed," mooed the clean, contented cows.) Then she ran across the neat vegetable patch, noting a lavender-bush at each corner — sure sign of a nice farmwife — and peeped into the dovecote. No dovecote is ever really quite tidy, owing to the habits of its occupants; Miss Bianca but paused on the threshold, and certainly didn't attempt the ladder leading to the first broad ledge behind the nesting-boxes; but the plump rows of sleeping doves looked in their way just as contented as the cows . . .

"This is evidently a very well-run farm indeed!" thought Miss Bianca.

In the house itself. she took the upstairs first, and within a matter of moments found the prettiest little bedroom imaginable.

Its windows were hung with buttercup-patterned chintz. A quilt in the same gay design covered a child-size bed. Upon the child-size dresser sat a whole row of dolls, just as though waiting for a little girl to come and play with them . . .

"Really quite ideal!" thought Miss Bianca.

The conversation overheard between the farmer and his wife amply confirmed this opinion; with a light heart Miss Bianca rejoined the Ambassador's party (again at the awkward turning by the oak tree), and thoroughly enjoyed the moonlight drive back.

Thus she had no difficulty at all — here we return to the General Meeting — in convincing even the male members present that the rescue of the child Patience could be safely undertaken without risk of having to lodge her behind the stove or go without Sunday dinner. As for the Ladies' Guild, they were even more determined to keep such a nice, rewarding adventure in their own hands.

"How I do pity that poor farmer and his wife," sighed the motherly mouse, "and what joy, girls, to think 'twill be we who restore their content!"

But as Bernard handed Miss Bianca from the platform, he gave her a very severe look.

3

"You might have been eaten by ferrets," said Bernard.

"I didn't go anywhere *near* ferrets," said Miss Bianca. "I didn't go into any woodland at all: just round the farm."

"Watchdogs, then," said Bernard gloomily. He was always more nervous for Miss Bianca than she was for herself.

"They don't keep a watchdog, I'm happy to say," retorted Miss Bianca. "Poor souls, hurling themselves against their collars all day long! It's quite pitiful to think of."

"I suppose if there *had* been a watchdog you'd have wanted the Prisoners' Aid Society to rescue *him*," said Bernard grimly. "I know you're not afraid of cats —" (this was a reference to their adventures in the Black Castle) — "but when it comes to pitying watchdogs, all reasonable limits are passed."

He spoke so crossly only because he was so devoted to her. Miss Bianca knew this, and gave him her sweetest smile before tripping off to head the supper table.

What a hubbub of animated conversation rose on every side! It was a peculiar source of pleasurable interest that the child Patience was bound for the Happy Valley, for though all present were city mice, nearly every family had country cousins: some merely exchanged Christmas cards, others were on picnicking terms, but there was no one unacquainted, if only by hearsay, with the Valley's delights. — A winter's supply left for the gleaning in each furrow! -- And what a motto that was, *Let nibble who needs!* More than one mouse was heard to regret that his parents had put him into a bank instead of on a farm — but they were just the ones who enjoyed talking about the Valley most, while rare is the masculine intelligence, however satisfied by retail trade, unresponsive to the charms of a combine-harvester. The Ladies' Guild dwelt chiefly upon home-cured bacon and fresh cheese and sausages not the shop sort; also upon buttercup-patterned curtains . . .

The menfolk's voices were louder, but just before coffee that of the games mistress topped them all.

Surveying the rows of empty dishes — so recently heaped with sardine tails in aspic and puffed wheat *au fromage,* let alone plain toast-crumbs —

"On a point of order, Madam Chairwoman!" cried the games mistress. "I suggest that upon the triumphal return of the Ladies' Guild from their heroic feat of rescue, it should be the *male* members of our Society who provide supper!"

Of course it wasn't a proper point of order, because the General Meeting was already ended. Miss Bianca, bowing to the spirit of the occasion, nonetheless took a show of hands.

By a narrow majority, the Ladies' Guild — as though in advance — proved triumphant!

POEM BY MISS BIANCA, WRITTEN THAT SAME NIGHT

How sad and lone sit farmer and his wife,
   How fond their thoughts of her who is no more!
Yet oh what happiness awaits them both,
   Greeting a new-found daughter at their door!

M. B.

3

The Ladies' Guild to the Rescue!

THE NEXT FEW days were the most exciting the
Ladies' Guild of the Prisoners' Aid Society had ever
known. The games mistress set up an assault course
in a disused attic, and classes rapidly formed for
training — up two chair rungs and down again, *up*
again and *down* again — "Don't weaken, girls!" cried
the games mistress — also with special emphasis on
skirt-climbing, the skirts represented by a pair of velvet
curtains left hanging over a clothes horse. It was far
more exciting than doing housework; many a husband
came home to find the table unlaid — his wife was
romping up chair rungs! No less pleasant was the
general burgeoning of community spirit: neighbors
who hadn't spoken to each other for weeks broke
silence to exchange their experiences — "Catches you
in the back, dear? With me it's behind the knees" —
or useful hints, such as put a pinch of table salt in the
bath, or always get a good grip on the hem.

Members too elderly for such violent exercise found almost equal satisfaction in preparing after-class snacks of competitive deliciousness, also in sewing neat arm-bands with P.A.S.L.G. on them. It was actually the mouse who'd offered Patience a home behind the stove who had the brilliant idea of fabricating scent-masks from strips of balloons.

"For what powerful perfumes, as is well known, don't ladies-in-waiting and such adorn their persons with?" she pointed out. "One whiff, very like, and no telling up from down!"

The little rubber masks were of all colors, pink and blue and yellow, just as the balloons burst and discarded by children are of all colors. Some mice looked so coquettish in them they had their photographs taken.

Naturally each class had a group photograph taken as well, with their armlets on and the games mistress in the middle.

Yet beneath all this surface frivolity purpose continued strong, and no class ever broke up without the singing of a brief anthem composed by Miss Bianca to a well-known air.

Shall little Patience be forgot
And never brought to mind?

We'll rout the Diamond Duchess yet
And show we're nae so blind!

But there was one thing about the Diamond Duchess's household that even Miss Bianca, perhaps fortunately, didn't know.

2

At last the great day dawned. — It was a Thursday, because Miss Bianca, though recognizing every member of the Ladies' Guild prepared to infiltrate the Diamond Palace on foot, felt they would stand a far better chance of all getting there together by public transport, and Thursday was when the municipal dust-cart went around.

Devoted Miss Bianca! Customarily she traveled by Diplomatic Bag in a Diplomatic airplane. At a pinch, she went first class (by train), in a reserved coupé, or by road in a Rolls-Royce. *She* could have gained the Palace simply by popping out of the Ambassadorial car as it drove by on its daily visit to the Chancellery. But like those other great leaders Napoleon and the Duke of Wellington, she scorned not to share the hardships of her troops.

"And we can put on our scent-masks straight away," said Miss Bianca to the games mistress.

The games mistress was second in command. Unlike Miss Bianca, she was very fond of giving orders. At her cry of "Scent-masks up!" all the members of the Ladies' Guild gathered waiting for the dust-cart hastily obeyed. Some had difficulty with the strings, but these Miss Bianca quietly helped, and then the games mistress counted them all up. — "Dear me, this is very curious!" said the games mistress. "There ought to be twenty-four — don't run about so, girls! — but I keep counting twenty-five. Who can the twenty-fifth be?"

In point of fact, it was Bernard.

So anxious was he for Miss Bianca, and so determined not to let her out of his sight again, he had actually attempted to disguise himself as a Lady. About his brawny right arm a circlet of sticky tape bore the letters P.A.S.L.G., his masculine features were shadowed by a bonnet out of the Boy Scouts' dressing-up box: it still wasn't a heavy enough disguise, once **she** got a good look at him, to deceive Miss Bianca! — Her nerves were naturally a little on edge; swiftly drawing him aside —

"My dear Bernard," said Miss Bianca, "how ridiculous you look!"

"I didn't mean to look ridiculous," said Bernard humbly. "I just meant to look like a member of the

33

Ladies' Guild. So that I could come with you."
Miss Bianca's nerves really *were* on edge.

"My dear Bernard," she repeated, more sharply,
"pray remember the dignity of a Secretary. Though
your solicitude is very touching, pray remember also
that this is not an expedition to any Black Castle!
The Diamond Palace, by your own account, is merely
an historic monument built in 1775. Now for good-
ness' sake take off that absurd bonnet and go home!"

At this moment the dust-cart loomed into view and
halted. Under the leadership of the games mistress,
up by wheel and trailing bucket every member of the
Ladies' Guild ran. To cries of "Where is Miss Bianca?"

up ran Miss Bianca too; and poor snubbed Bernard was left behind.

He hadn't even deceived the games mistress.

"Silly mistake, that of mine," said the games mistress. "And I must say I think it was jolly decent of the Secretary, to come and see us off . . ."

3

On the dust-cart rolled with its devoted cargo — twenty-four members of the Ladies' Guild, each wearing armlet and scent-mask. Pink and blue and yellow, a positive nosegay of bright colors displayed each group, as it sat (holding hands) between the horrid garbage bags. Only Miss Bianca's mask was black, fabricated from oiled silk, so that all might recognize and follow her. — Actually her ermine coat alone would have sufficed, but she was not beyond coquetry, and knew how wonderfully becoming was black silk against silvery fur. In fact it was a rather coquettish-looking party altogether. But not on that account did the spirit of heroism burn less bright in any breast. On the contrary: to be looking one's best, as every female knows, helps one to *be* one's best . . .

The dust-cart rumbled on, picking up the early-morning detritus of the city. None of it was very nice:

discarded fish-and-chip papers made the scent-masks a sheer necessity: even despite them the aroma from an empty beer bottle nearly asphyxiated the games mistress, and only the devoted efforts of her prize class saved her, by holding her head out over the tailboard until she recovered. It was a very exciting incident — as were no less the incidents of the bent fork, the broken jam jar and the dead kitten. This last — all feuds forgotten under the shadow of the Grim Reaper — the Ladies' Guild interred as neatly as possible under potato peelings, while Miss Bianca said a few appropriate words.

Actually the journey took all day, because the city had only one dust-cart, so it had to go all round. (The City Fathers were so conceited, they spent all the city money putting up showy monuments to themselves.) But a late arrival at the Diamond Palace was part of Miss Bianca's plan, and the Ladies' Guild had brought picnic lunches. These made a really nice funeral-feast for the dead kitten, after which all took naps, and then Miss Bianca employed the rest of the time in a final briefing.

"The Duchess having held her Evening Circle in her State Saloon," explained Miss Bianca, "all her ladies will naturally attend her to her bedchamber . . ."

Miss Bianca's familiarity with the domestic habits of the aristocracy, and Court etiquette in general, always quite fascinated the Ladies' Guild. They listened with rapt attention.

". . . the child Patience of course being with them," continued Miss Bianca, "in her quality of Tirewoman; and there they will remain until their mistress is asleep. *We* shall not meet the Duchess at all."

Several members actually objected that they'd *like* to! — such was the mounting spirit of heroism!

"Personally I prefer not to make the acquaintance," said Miss Bianca coolly (and thus impressing her followers afresh). "What is equally to the point, no more shall we encounter the Duchess's Major-domo — naturally excluded from the bedchamber by his sex. The only members of the Household *we* shall encounter are the Duchess's ladies-in-waiting, as they re-emerge, Patience among them, through the State Saloon."

"And that's when we up and at 'em?" cried the games mistress eagerly.

"Precisely so!" said Miss Bianca.

"And carry away the poor child," cried the motherly mouse, "and all subscribe for her coach fare to the Happy Valley?"

"Precisely so!" agreed Miss Bianca.

"Mightn't she just come and sup with us first — just to show the menfolk?" cried another mouse.

"I'm sure she'll be delighted to!" smiled Miss Bianca.

In such happy plans the last stages of the journey seemed to pass quite quickly, and it was with one enthusiastic voice, as the Diamond Palace at last loomed into view, that all the Ladies' Guild shouted out:

"There it is!"

There it was indeed.

4

The Diamond Palace

IT GLITTERED LIKE an iceberg — as huge, and bright, and beautiful, and cold.

It was strange. The Diamond Palace was so beautiful, tourists came from all parts of the world in coachloads to admire just the sparkling balustrades and balconies, turrets and minarets, that could be seen towering above the outer wall. To make out the more elaborate traceries on the upper pinnacles they had to use field glasses — sun glasses too, in fine weather, when each rock-crystal facet caught and flung back the sun rays like the facet of a prism. All the tourists saw of the Diamond Palace was its top part, yet they compared it favorably with Blenheim, Versailles and the Taj Mahal. The strange thing was that however pleased they felt to have beheld such a sight, and however hot the day, as their coaches bore them on again they felt, also, cold.

Inside, it was cold indeed.

Icy-cold.

Diamond-cold.

A child's hands were ice-cold always, polishing the diamond figurines in the great glass cases, and the big diamond drops of the lustres, and the innumerable lesser diamonds with which every single piece of furniture was studded.

But if you didn't polish properly, you were whipped . . .

Perhaps something of this penetrated even to the tourists in their coaches.

2

Descending from the dust-cart, however, and as they crept in file under the sill of the back door, the members of the Ladies' Guild were still too hot with excitement to be affected. One or two of the more sensitive attributed a slight shiver to nerves, while Miss Bianca herself shivered simply — or so she thought — with repugnance at being set down at a tradesmen's entrance. "But such is a dust-cart's nature!" she recognized sensibly. As for the other mice, gazing up at the arches of a mere pantry, and at the even greater arches (as they crept into the kitchen) above the enormous ovens, they imagined themselves in the State Saloon already!

To be sure, there wasn't any smell of cooking; nor any clatter — indeed more probable, considering the lateness of the hour — of washing-up.

"Strange!" thought Miss Bianca to herself. "With such an establishment — for each lady-in-waiting, of whom I have heard there are a dozen, will surely have a maid, and that makes twenty-four persons dining at least — one wouldn't expect everything in order quite so soon? Yet here is not even a scullion still at work!"

She kept her own counsel, however, and merely observed that State Saloons were usually upstairs.

"Through that baize door, don't you think?" suggested Miss Bianca. "Through that baize door and then probably up a Grand Staircase . . ."

Of course she was used to palaces, and it was fortunate the mice had her for leader, otherwise they might have lost themselves irretrievably just in the rock-crystal basement. But under Miss Bianca's guidance every right corridor was safely followed, and every wrong door safely passed —

"But I think I'll just look into the Steward's Room!" said Miss Bianca.

She slipped under the sill. There at his desk snored

the Duchess's Major-domo, his head pillowed on his arms beside a bottle of port. Much as she reprobated excessive drinking, Miss Bianca nodded with satisfaction! — then on she led the Ladies' Guild again, now up the right service-stair, until at last all emerged in good order on the ground floor.

Here there was a brief pause to get their breaths back — not only from their exertions, but before the splendors of the Grand Staircase!

It rose in an enormous double sweep, like a horseshoe, from the main entrance hall below to an arcaded gallery above. Every inch of balustrading (Greek-key pattern) was thick with diamonds. So were the stair rods holding down the cloth-of-gold carpet. — Miss Bianca set foot upon it as negligently, and ran up it as lightly, as if it had been mere drugget.

Yet even the splendors of the Grand Staircase paled before the splendors of the State Saloon.

Here the floor was so vast, the mice could scarcely see the farther end. From the ceiling hung six great diamond chandeliers of unexampled brilliance. In cabinets ranged round the walls diamond-studded *objets d'art* glittered through the glass like frost under a December sun; while from a central dais blazed the most dazzling object of all — the Grand Duchess's throne!

This was carved in the shape of two dragons supporting between them a seat of stretched sharkskin. The four diamonds set as their eyes were the size of walnuts. In front of the throne stood a sharkskin footstool coiled about by a diamond snake . . .

Personally Miss Bianca thought it all extremely vulgar. But as she glanced back over the awestruck ranks behind her she recognized this was no moment to give a talk on good taste in interior decoration. Far more immediately useful (and in any case there was no danger of mice buying themselves diamond chandeliers, even on hire-purchase) was to pretend to be equally impressed.

"Stupendous!" exclaimed Miss Bianca. "Really quite stupendous! I don't remember ever seeing anything quite like it."

Several members of the Ladies' Guild murmured that no more did they.

"Which makes it all the more extraordinary," mused Miss Bianca, as though to herself but still loud enough to be overheard, "to think that within an hour at most these splendid halls will be the scene of our humble Society's triumph! — The disarray of the Duchess's ladies," exclaimed Miss Bianca, more loudly, "the leading forth to freedom of the child Patience — such scenes as *those* I'm sure these halls have *never* witnessed! What a blessing indeed that the eyes of the Ladies' Guild are neither dazzled by diamonds nor dismayed by dragons, but see only the clear light of Duty!"

Her words acted on her followers just as tonically as she had intended. They burst into such prolonged cheering, the games mistress had to shush them. Then, with renewed confidence, at Miss Bianca's directions, all scattered behind and beneath the cabinets round the walls, ready at her signal to rush forth as soon as the ladies-in-waiting, and the child Patience, appeared.

Miss Bianca herself took up station under the Duchess's very footstool. — If she shivered again, she thought it was just because it was a footstool in such horribly bad taste.

Indeed, Miss Bianca was feeling every moment more and more confident. All was evidently just as she had foreseen: the Duchess's ladies and the child Patience still within the Duchess's bedchamber waiting for the Duchess to fall asleep, the Duchess's Major-domo most obviously off duty; all things considered, when Miss Bianca pictured the rout of those mouse-harried ladies, her only slight anxiety was a rather snobbish one . . .

"Games mistress!" called Miss Bianca softly.

"Ma'am!" replied the games mistress — leaping out from behind a cabinet and springing to unnecessary attention.

"If the more active *rôle* appeals to you," murmured Miss Bianca, "and if while *I* but take charge of the child, *you* will lead forth our members to harry the ladies-in-waiting —"

"You bet it appeals to me!" cried the games mistress.

"Then perhaps you would be so good as to harry them down the Grand Staircase towards the front door."

It wasn't entirely snobbishness. Miss Bianca had willingly *infiltrated* the Diamond Palace by the trades-men's entrance. Quite apart from her personal re-pugnance to dust-bins, she felt that the child Patience's first steps to freedom deserved to cross a more worthy sill, and so wanted to make sure *which* door the ladies-in-waiting flung open first.

"Leave it to me, ma'am!" cried the games mistress. "The front door it shall be!"

But there was still something even Miss Bianca, let alone the Ladies' Guild, didn't know, about the Duchess's household.

They were soon to find out.

3

Suddenly a door opposite the dais opened. Through it, in two lines of six each, the Duchess's ladies-in-waiting filed. Their tall erect figures, from sweeping velvet skirt to nodding ostrich plume, were so accurately reflected in the rock-crystal floor, there seemed indeed not twelve but twenty-four of them. But did the brave Ladies' Guild on that account quail? No!

"Up, girls, and at 'em!" shrieked the games mistress.

Forth rushed all the Ladies' Guild squeaking like little railway engines. Recklessly they advanced upon the velvet hems . . .

Which swept on as smoothly and mechanically as before.

Even the one the games mistress had her teeth into.

Within a matter of seconds it was all too dreadfully apparent that the Duchess's ladies-in-waiting, far from jumping on chairs, had no fear of mice whatever!

In fact — as this alone would have sufficed to demonstrate — they weren't real ladies-in-waiting at all, but some sort of dreadful, inhuman, clockwork monsters . . .

5

The Awful Truth

NOT BECAUSE SHE was a witch did the Grand Duchess choose to be so served: but because she was worse than a witch. The rumors of witchcraft that hung about her name were at once ill-merited and above her deserts. Most witches are such humble folk, a little magic (black or white) gives them their only importance. The Duchess, rich and powerful from birth, simply gave rein to a completely odious nature.

Once there had been proper ladies-in-waiting in the Diamond Palace; but so autocratic was her temper, not even the meekest could avoid displeasing her. If this one smiled, the Grand Duchess took it for mockery; another who looked grave would be accused of sulking. A third who tried to make light conversation would be called a chattering parrot; a fourth who prudently held her tongue, a dumb beast. Nor did the Duchess's selfish tyranny stop at mere abuse; herself seated on a cushioned throne, she kept the ladies standing all day long — not the slightest movement allowed save for a deep curtsey every quarter of an hour; on the hour itself, they had to curtsey as many times as the clock struck, for this was the way the Duchess liked to tell the time. Poor ladies — afraid to speak, afraid to be silent; afraid to smile, afraid to frown; afraid even to *sit down!* Yet because each had been chosen for her extreme docility and high sense of duty, they bore it; until one midnight, when no fewer than six fell in faints, the Duchess screamed that they did it on purpose and dismissed them all.

"Find me ladies who won't faint after even *forty-eight* hours!" screamed the Duchess to her Major-domo. "And who'll neither keep silent nor say anything I don't want to hear!"

The Major-domo, who was a very clever man, thought for three days (while the Duchess stayed in bed), and then went to a friend of his who was a very clever clockwork-maker. When another three days later the Duchess got up, there in her antechamber stood the most perfect lady-in-waiting ever seen. Upon the Duchess's approach she sank into a deep curtsey; then rose to stand as perfectly motionless as before. Not a finger-tip stirred, nor a hair!

"Humph," said the Duchess.

"As your Grace pleases," said the lady-in-waiting.

"Can you stand like that four times round the clock?" asked the Duchess suspiciously.

"As your Grace pleases," said the lady-in-waiting.

"Humph," said the Duchess again. "You're a bit monotonous, but those happen to be the only words I like to hear. — Engage her," she added, to the Major-domo.

"Of course your Grace has observed," said the Major-

domo rather nervously, "naturally your Grace's exquisite powers of observation have not failed to remark,
that the lady is in fact a mechanical figure . . ."

"She is, is she? No, I hadn't," said the Duchess.
"All the better! — order eleven more like her."

So the Major-domo ordered eleven more.

There were still some things, however, the mechanical ladies-in-waiting couldn't do. They couldn't for
instance, put the Duchess's shoes on for her in the
morning, or put her wig away at night. (She was far
too proud ever to do anything for herself.) They
couldn't polish all the diamond ornaments in the
State Saloon. Worst of all, they couldn't flinch when
reprimanded, or burst into tears when told how stupid
they were. There was something to be said for human
beings after all, decided the Duchess! — and determined upon engaging just one more, a very small and
weak specimen, whom she could make cry whenever
she pleased, besides having her shoes and wig and
ornaments attended to.

Thus it was that whenever the news of an orphaned
girl-child reached his ears, the Major-domo at once
sent out his spies to kidnap her. Patience was but the
last of a series, all the others having died young.

What a life poor Patience led! — polishing all day
long, with ice-cold fingers, when she wasn't running

at the cruel Duchess's beck and call! Putting on the
Duchess's shoes each morning was bad enough —
stuffing the Duchess's big gouty toes under the big
diamond buckles, and being rapped on the wrist
whenever the Duchess felt a twinge! — but even
worse was putting the Duchess's wig away each night.
It was a horrible wig, never combed from year's end
to year's end: the pomaded curls just grew greasier
and greasier, and the big diamond stars in it dirtier
and dirtier, until handling it was like handling a
greasy hedgehog. Patience never once managed to set
it on its stand without getting her fingers pricked, as
the blood spots on her one-and-only handkerchief bore
witness . . .

Worst of all, just as Miss Bianca told the General
Meeting, was the deprivation of all affection.

The child instinctively sought even a simulacrum
of it. Very late one night (after putting the Duchess's
wig away), she found one of the Duchess's ladies
standing alone in the Duchess's closet. — There was
nothing particular in that: she was the lady on night
duty. Nor could Patience normally have distinguished
her from any of the other ladies, save by her gown of
carnation velvet. But away from the diamond chandeliers of the State Saloon some trick of gentler light,
through the closet window, made the enameled face

look for once almost human — and almost kind. Patience ran up close and caught a fold of the carnation skirt between her hands.

"Oh, please won't you talk to me a little?" she begged. "I'm so lonely! I don't ask anything more — I know it would be as much as your place is worth — but if you'd only just talk to me a little, couldn't we almost be friends?" pleaded Patience. "I need a friend so badly!"

She paused; for it seemed the lady was really about to answer.

So she did — though first, as the clock struck one, sinking into a deep curtsey.

"As your Grace pleases!" replied the lady-in-waiting.

"Oh, don't say that to *me*," begged Patience. "I'm not the Duchess! Just say something you'd say to a little girl!"

"As your Grace pleases," said the lady-in-waiting.

For once something must have gone wrong with her mechanism. As Patience still knelt half incredulous, still pressing a fold of carnation velvet to her cheek, the high inhuman voice whirred into repetition.

"*As your Grace pleases, as your Grace pleases, as your Grace pleases . . .*"

2

What could the simple though devoted Ladies' Guild do against such monsters as these? Alas, it was the *Ladies' Guild* that ran!

As the sweeping skirts mechanically advanced, half the members were in retreat already — even before a pair of steely shoes began to stamp and click beneath that same carnation velvet hem. The sound, so precisely like that made by the spring of a mousetrap, completed the disarray of all — and helter-skelter higgledy-piggledy tripping and squeaking and slipping and squealing away all the Ladies' Guild ran just as fast as ever they could!

All save Miss Bianca.

When the ladies-in-waiting at last halted, drawn up in a semicircle round the Duchess's throne, there were left confronting each other just Miss Bianca and a little girl.

She was a very little girl. Although to Miss Bianca's certain knowledge eight years old, she looked no more than five or six, she was so pitifully undernourished. Her little thin arms, her little thin neck, were blue with cold. Elf-locks of pale gold hair, that should have been brushed to prettiness, hung in wisps about her

pale, hollow cheeks. She looked like a neglected little scarecrow. But that she had once been nicely brought up was apparent from her very first words.

"Poor little things!" said the child Patience. "Poor little mice! I do hope they all get safe home!"

"Do not doubt of it," said Miss Bianca rather bitterly, "under the leadership of the games mistress!" — She checked herself. Why shouldn't the Ladies' Guild run for home? Indeed, wasn't it their *duty* to run for home — their valiant, well-intentioned efforts having so obviously failed? They had their families to think of . . . "They have their families to think of," explained Miss Bianca.

"How lovely!" sighed the child Patience. "But are *you* going to *stay?*" she added eagerly.

Miss Bianca hesitated. She glanced swiftly towards the ranks of ladies-in-waiting. They were now standing quite still. It didn't make them much less frightening, but at least they were standing still. — Could it be possible, thought Miss Bianca, that her plan was still viable after all? — and that some means of exit could be flung open, if not by the ladies, then by the child Patience herself?

"Can you open the front door, my dear child?" asked Miss Bianca.

"Oh, no," said Patience. "Why, *that's* never opened at all!"

"Then the back door?" suggested Miss Bianca bravely.

"That's kept locked too," said Patience, "and I don't know where the key is. — Oh, do *please* say you'll stay with me, and be my friend!"

She pressed her little thin hands together beseechingly. Down each thin cheek, in her earnestness and anxiety, the tears began to trickle. It was an appeal impossible (at least to Miss Bianca) to resist.

"Until we both leave together!" promised Miss Bianca.

3

She spoke more stoutly than she felt. As the child carried her up to a little attic bedroom — up winding rock-crystal stairs innumerable, along a last winding rock-crystal corridor — Miss Bianca felt a chill to her marrow. "Can those things outside the window be *icicles?*" inquired Miss Bianca. "No," said Patience, "just horrid rock-crystal carvings." "But all these lumps of ice on your bedstead?" asked Miss Bianca. "Oh, *they're* just diamonds," said Patience, "and you

can't think how uncomfortable! But won't you please
get in beside me all the same?"

Into bed she crept, just taking off her frock first.
(The poor child, Miss Bianca noted, hadn't even a
nightgown. What was even worse, she hadn't even a
toothbrush. For all toilet she just dipped a torn old
rag into a jar of cold water.) Miss Bianca, herself ac-

customed to nightly massaging with eau de Cologne,
still curled up on the thin pillow with her usual grace.
— It wasn't she but the child Patience who tossed and
turned, and who from each first brief dream woke so
pitifully sobbing. "No doubt it is in her dreams she
remembers most," thought Miss Bianca compassion-
ately, "of all the affection she once enjoyed . . ."

"Try and lie still," said Miss Bianca gently. "Would
you like me to sing you to sleep?"

"Oh, yes please," said Patience. "Long ago, when I
was just a little girl, I remember being sung to sleep
every night . . ."

So in her sweetest, most silvery tones Miss Bianca
began to sing a lullaby:

Long, long ago and lemon trees and lilacs,
*   Long, long ago and lily bud and leaf,*
Two turtle doves lived in an old, old elm tree
*   Far away from sorrow, far away from grief.*
Oh lemon trees and lullaby, oh lavender and lilac,
Oh long ago and lullaby and lily bud and leaf!

She had to sing it three times over, the first two
because Patience liked it so much, and the third while
the child's tear-wet lashes shut quite tight, and with
her cheek still nestled against Miss Bianca's soft cool
fur, she fell fast asleep.

4

Miss Bianca stayed awake much longer.

It wasn't only from cramp (if she moved, she was afraid of disturbing Patience), nor because a diamond-studded bed is so uncomfortable. (Miss Bianca's delicate frame felt every knobble through the pillow as accurately as a certain Princess once felt a pea through seven mattresses.) Mental distress alone would have destroyed Miss Bianca's repose even in her own Porcelain Pagoda.

For the more she contemplated the situation, the more uncomfortable *it* appeared too — the Ladies' Guild utterly routed, herself left but a fellow captive in the Diamond Palace with the very prisoner they should have rescued — and surrounded by mechanical ladies-in-waiting!

To be truthful, the mechanical ladies-in-waiting, though *she* hadn't run away from them, really frightened her. Miss Bianca hadn't been afraid of the jailers in the Black Castle — they, however cruel and odious, had at least been *natural,* as cats are natural, or ferrets, or any other traditional enemy of mice. But when she recalled the cold, inhuman bearing of the Duchess's ladies-in-waiting, Miss Bianca shuddered as before witchcraft indeed . . .

"If only the Ladies' Guild puts in a proper report!" thought Miss Bianca. "If only *Bernard* knows!"

But alas, the memory of Bernard didn't make her feel better, it made her feel worse.

"Oh that I had not spoken so harshly to him!" Miss Bianca now reproached herself — recalling Bernard's honest features beneath the borrowed bonnet, and the hurt expression on them as she chid him and turned away. "How unkind I was," sighed Miss Bianca, "and even worse, how impolite!"

She who so rarely failed in courtesy and understanding now paid almost too hardly for a single lapse. It was really quite pardonable — her nerves so naturally on edge, at that moment of waiting for the dust-cart — but now, in the small hours after midnight, when everything always looks blackest, she felt Bernard would be thoroughly justified in abandoning her forever and perhaps even helping to vote the games mistress into her place as Madam Chairwoman . . .

A second, deeper sigh agitated Miss Bianca's breast. — The sound, slight as it was, penetrated her companion's uneasy slumber.

"Are *you* unhappy too?" asked Patience drowsily.

At least Miss Bianca wouldn't fail in courtesy again!

"Not at all, my dear child," she said cheerfully,

"with such a nice little friend as yourself to bear me company!"

She composed herself afresh, taking care that her smooth cool fur still brushed Patience's cheek like a good-night kiss. Both slept at last — as around them the whole cruel, cold Diamond Palace slept. The child Patience and Miss Bianca made but a very small kernel of warmth and affection at its cold, cruel heart.

6

Back at the Moot-hall

MEANWHILE THE DEFEATED Ladies' Guild had naturally made the best of things. Who could blame them — their menfolk awaiting their return only too ready to make the *worst*?

The games mistress took charge. It was she who got them all out again from the Diamond Palace. She had in her time organized so many paper-chases and treasure-hunts and such for the Boy Scouts, she remembered every step of the way back from the Grand Staircase to the tradesmen's entrance; whence (having checked each member in turn under the sill) she marshaled them all onto a late-night bus for newspaper staffs, which passed actually by the cellars in which the Moot-hall stood.

Here, before entering, she again called a hasty roll to make sure no one was missing — as, with the unfortunate exception of Miss Bianca, no one was — and made them tidy themselves up. "Right turn and

brush the back in front!" cried the games mistress.
"Comb whiskers and adjust arm-bands!" When this
had been done at least the members of the Ladies'
Guild didn't *look* defeated. In fact, as they marched
into the Hall with the games mistress at their head —
"Ears up, girls!" — they looked so smart and appar-
ently victorious that every husband, son and brother
rose spontaneously to his feet.

"Reporting to the Prisoners' Aid Society and Com-
mittee," called the games mistress loudly, "the Prisoners' Aid Society Ladies' Guild is happy to announce
jolly nearly complete success!"

There was an immediate, and generous, burst of
cheering, led by Bernard on the platform. Cries of
"Good old Mum!" "Hip hip for Auntie!" and "Well
done the missus!" shook the rafters.

"Indeed I think we *have* done well," said the games mistress modestly. "The confusion created no one who wasn't there could believe! As for the child herself —"

Here she paused, because this was where things were getting tricky, also there was a general rush for the door — bench after bench rapidly emptying as their occupants hurried out to take a look at Patience for themselves: whom they naturally expected, after the games mistress's words, to find just outside. (She wouldn't be able to get *in,* on account of her size.)

Among the first was the old Professor of Mathematics. He returned wearing an expression the games mistress didn't like at all.

"Hum," said he. "Not there. Where exactly *is* the child?"

There was a dead silence. Bernard on the platform stood up and scanned the ranks of the Ladies' Guild with growing anxiety. Up till then, when he didn't see Miss Bianca among them, he had assumed her modestly allowing the Guild its moment of glory — or possibly staying outside with Patience to lend the child moral support, and possibly coach her in a little speech of thanks . . .

"Is she perhaps already in the Happy Valley?" inquired the Professor.

"Well, not exactly," said the games mistress.

"Or on her way to it?"

"Not exactly either," admitted the games mistress. "In fact, she's still in the Diamond Palace . . ."

"AND WHERE IS MISS BIANCA?" shouted Bernard.

"Well, she's in the Diamond Palace too," admitted the games mistress.

A couple of pot plants went for six as Bernard rushed to the platform's edge.

"You mean you *left* her?"

How often had the games mistress pulled a hockey match out of the fire in the last moments of play! She was famous for it.

"Not at all; she *stayed*," corrected the games mistress. "Personally I thought it a jolly good show. — And now I'm sure we all deserve a jolly good supper," she added briskly, "which I only hope the men haven't forgotten to provide!"

2

Actually the men had neither forgotten *nor* provided it — that is, in the sense of preparing anything themselves; they had just hired a catering firm, with the happy result that it really *was* a good supper. Cold bacon-rinds *à la souris* neighbored sardine-bones deviled and whole whitebaits in aspic. The center-piece was a marshmallow studded with grape pips, while to drink there was elderberry wine, or sink water for the teetotalers, both ad lib.

Again (so swiftly can appetite obliterate the higher instincts) the very same cries resounded, of "Hip hip for Auntie!" and "Good old Mum!" as the mice set to. Even the Professor of Mathematics didn't disdain such a feast: he tucked into whitebait with the youngest.

His quaffing of elderberry wine even set them a bad example!

Only one seat remained vacant: Miss Bianca's; and halfway through, Bernard's.

3

Small heart had Bernard for festivity; he slipped away as soon as he decently could. He knew there was no hope, just then, of getting any sense out of the Ladies' Guild — and indeed when he saw how soon their whiskers began to droop again, and their coats to stare, he lacked the harshness even to attempt it.

After all, they'd *tried:* had performed (for *them,* so unused to adventures) genuine feats of heroism; and if they were now making the best of things — who could blame them?

But alone in his bachelor quarters Bernard paced the floor far into the night.

7

The Grand Duchess

SADLY ENOUGH HAD Miss Bianca and the child
Patience fallen asleep: to what perils did they not
awake!

But when Patience saw Miss Bianca on her pillow,
she smiled for the first time in months.

"Oh, how lovely!" she exclaimed. "I thought you
were a dream!"

"Certainly not," said Miss Bianca — feeling it high
time to introduce herself. "I am Miss Bianca."

If this didn't make quite the usual impression, it
was because Patience had led such a secluded life;
Miss Bianca readily forgave the childish ignorance.

"How pretty!" cried Patience. "I shall love to have
a friend with such a pretty name! — And are we
really going to leave this horrid place together, just
as you told me last night?"

Miss Bianca was feeling so much better (as people
usually do in the morning), and in fact so sure that

Bernard *wouldn't* abandon her (a belief, as has been seen, fully justified), she nodded quite cheerfully.

"At the earliest opportunity," she promised. "Until when, you must do nothing to arouse suspicion, but go about your duties in the usual way. What are your first duties?"

Patience, wriggling into her dress, sighed.

"First I polish in the State Saloon, then I go and put the Duchess's shoes on for her, and her dreadful, horrible wig, and then there's the Morning Levée —"

"Ah!" said Miss Bianca. "I believe I shall attend it."

To be truthful again, and this time it does Miss Bianca nothing but credit, she made the decision purely as a test of courage. She was entirely *blasée* about Levées and Duchesses, and certainly had no wish even to appear to be paying respects to such an evidently odious and vulgar Duchess as this one was. Miss Bianca would truly have preferred to remain secluded in the attic and not set eyes on the Grand Duchess at all. But she *had*, during the night, admitted herself frightened — of the mechanical ladies-in-waiting. Fear was an emotion Miss Bianca despised; and now that she was herself again, felt it would be impossible to quit the Diamond Palace with such a stain on her honor. So she resolved to wipe it out by confronting the monsters once more.

She made her usual careful toilet — indeed taking so long over it, Patience was forced to run off. For Courts are Courts, however *outré,* and simply to show her own good breeding Miss Bianca took rather special pains with the gloss of her coat and the set of her whiskers. She spent an hour rubbing up her silver chain, until it shone — not like diamonds! Dear me, no! — but like a very fine thread of moonshine. Then she made her way to the State Saloon.

2

Patience was already gone to attend the Duchess's toilet. But the ladies were there.

Still drawn up in a semicircle before the hideous throne. They hadn't stirred all night!

Miss Bianca advanced towards them. — Not a finger now moved, nor the toe of a shoe!

"Evidently 'twas but a faulty mechanism," thought Miss Bianca, pausing by the figure in carnation velvet, "that made her stamp so!"

She walked all the way round. Carnation, orange, purple — peacock and green and yellow and scarlet — glowed the velvet skirts; heavy too with gold embroideries, and stiffened by buckram petticoats. "Certainly they make a fine show!" thought Miss Bianca.

But not a hem lifted, not a heel clicked. "What simpletons we were," thought Miss Bianca, "myself no less than the Ladies' Guild, to feel fear of such mere, if expensive, effigies!"

Just at that moment the air grew perceptibly colder.

"This is really the draftiest palace I ever entered!" thought Miss Bianca, still in a spirit of criticism. — Or rather, *began* to think; because just the next moment the door opposite the dais opened to admit first the Duchess's Majo-domo, then the child Patience, then the Grand Duchess herself.

Courageous as she was, and sophisticated as she was — and no longer afraid of the ladies-in-waiting as she was — at her first glimpse of that tall dreadful figure, Miss Bianca felt suddenly too cold to think properly at all.

3

Very tall indeed was the Grand Duchess: taller even than her ladies, and gaunt as a gallows. The dirty stars in her wig seemed at least six feet from the ground. They were not the only diamonds she carried; big necklaces and chatelaines of diamonds clanked from bosom and waist down to the big diamond buckles on her shoes. The brilliant set in the

crook of her cane was bigger even than those set for eyes in the heads of the dragons supporting her throne.

If Miss Bianca noticed all these details first, it was because even she flinched a moment, before looking at the Duchess's face.

One glance, and she looked away again; from a countenance that might have been carved by some gargoyle-maker, as grotesque as evil, inhuman in its stoniness, yet marked too by the (worst) human traits of arrogance, selfishness and cruelty. Deep furrows of anger barred the forehead; out from each nostril flared the lines of pride; cruelty itself, about the mouth, grimaced triumphant. "No wonder," thought Miss Bianca incoherently, "the air is so cold!" — and she shivered uncontrollably.

Slowly, between the ranks of her ladies, stalked the Duchess — kicking contemptuously at them as she passed.

"And what d'you say to *that,* my ladies?" inquired the Grand Duchess sardonically.

With one whirring mechanical voice —

"*As your Grace pleases!*" answered all the mechanical ladies-in-waiting.

"Very proper," grinned the Duchess, seating herself on her throne, "if a trifle monotonous! And now what does the *child* say — who hasn't placed my footstool?"

"Please, your Grace, I — I was only waiting for your Grace to sit," stammered Patience.

As she pulled the footstool into place, down whipped the Duchess's cane across her wrist; she couldn't help but cry out.

"Even better!" grinned the Duchess. "The human note! — Don't you agree, you old fool?"

"Certainly, your Grace!" fawned the Major-domo. "A very human note indeed! I selected the child specially on account of it."

"Then we'll hear it again!" snarled the Grand Duchess.

Never before had Miss Bianca suffered the indignity of being struck — even vicariously. For the second time she flinched, as the child Patience flinched. She was all this time sheltered beneath one of the velvet skirts, and evidently unobserved; she was in no immediate personal danger. But every nerve in her body quivered nonetheless; and as she again forced herself to look into that cruel, lowering, diamond-starred-about visage, she felt quite numbed before such a force of wickedness as even the Black Castle had not prepared her for.

"Oh that we were in the power of but a simple

witch!" thought Miss Bianca. "Oh Bernard," she added mentally, "pray come quickly! — If I have ever underestimated your humble, beautiful nature, pray forgive me and *come at once!*"

4

But that day passed, and the next, and the next: no Bernard.

No fresh rescue party from the Prisoners' Aid Society — not even a postcard from the Ladies' Guild: nothing.

The reasons for this were rather complicated. Let it not be supposed that the Society regarded the loss of its Chairwoman as a bagatelle. Encomiums of Miss Bianca's kindness in remaining at the side of the child Patience took priority on every next agenda at every next General Meeting, also several resolutions were passed affirming complete faith in her. In a way, the Society had only too *much* faith in Miss Bianca — and while planning in detail the gala supper to celebrate her return, gave no thought as to when, and still less as to *whether,* that return might be expected.

All save Bernard; and Bernard's difficulty was that he still couldn't find out exactly what had *happened* in the Diamond Palace. The Ladies' Guild indeed now talked freely enough about their adventures there — but only up to a point. They quite reveled in descriptions of diamond chandeliers, and Grand Staircases, and State Saloons, but when it came to the crucial point of why Patience (and so Miss Bianca) had been left behind, no one seemed to remember anything at all. Secretly, of course, they were a little ashamed of themselves, and to cover this guilty feeling a theory somehow grew up that Miss Bianca had rather encouraged Patience to stay on, just for a few days, so that she could stay too as Patience's guest.

"After all, old man," said the games mistress, "Miss Bianca, let's face it, does rather *like* Palaces. It's only natural, moving in Embassy circles as she does: personally I've always thought it jolly decent of her to act as our Chairwoman at all."

Bernard listened uneasily. To a mouse of his particularly humble (and beautiful) nature it all sounded quite possible: devoted as he was to Miss Bianca, he had never thoroughly understood a character so much more sophisticated, and the idea that a Diamond Palace could be positive anathema to her never occurred to him. He just thought that as Miss Bianca was so much the most beautiful of mice, such a beautifulest palace was but a fit setting for her, and one she would naturally enjoy.

"So if *I* were you, old man," said the games mistress bracingly, "I'd just wait until she decides her leave's up from the Embassy, and comes tripping back with the child of her own accord!"

It all sounded quite reasonable to Bernard. He still paced the floor each night (wearing quite a track in his stamp-paper carpet), but he didn't do anything. He was too confused.

"Oh Miss Bianca," thought Bernard confusedly, "if you aren't in deadly peril, I do hope you're enjoying yourself!"

8

The Captives

ENJOYING HERSELF! Poor Miss Bianca, who never in all her life had been so miserable as amid the cold, cruel splendors of the Diamond Palace!

The Major-domo's name was Mandrake. He had once committed a very wicked crime, of which only the Duchess now had evidence. Thus he was as much her slave as the mechanical ladies-in-waiting — and had to work much harder! There was only he to prepare, in the deserted kitchens, out of an enormous Deepfreeze, the Duchess's daily food of pheasant, or partridge, or jugged hare — her tastes ran strictly to game — as there was only Patience to attend the Duchess's toilet. Mandrake even had to put out the garbage, since he dared not trust Patience to unlock the back door; and all this so embittered a temperament already harsh and morose, his only relaxation when off duty was to sit alone in the steward's room (as Miss Bianca had observed him), drinking bad port.

In the stables, a couple of wall-eyed old coach-horses were carelessly fed, and still more carelessly groomed, by a couple of dissolute ostlers — both, like Mandrake, with criminal records. (Even the two horses had criminal records: each having once kicked a man to death.) But the stables were quite separate from the rest of the Palace, and no rumor of human jollity (however dissolute) ever penetrated therefrom to challenge, even momentarily, the mechanical voices of the mechanical ladies-in-waiting.

"*As your Grace pleases, as your Grace pleases, as your Grace pleases . . .*"

It made no difference whether it was the Duchess who addressed them, or Mandrake who in passing uttered a bitter oath, or the child Patience a piteous sigh. "*As your Grace pleases!*" answered the mechanical ladies; just as whether the Duchess observed them or not they curtseyed once at every quarter, and then again to the strokes of the hour. Thus the Grand Duchess's dreadful, cold-dispensing presence could never be forgotten, even when out of reach of her cane.

Miss Bianca helped Patience with the polishing.

Her tiny fingers could explore where even a child's hands couldn't: never had the ornaments in the State Saloon gleamed brighter! But Patience was rapped across the wrist no less often for that.

They made their scanty meals from the Duchess's leavings. Patience almost starved from lack of nourishment — and Miss Bianca from pride. There was plenty left for a mouse, on each pheasant or partridge bone! — but Miss Bianca, discovering that the Duchess never touched her roll, preferred a farinaceous diet; and even so nibbled just enough each day to sustain the vital spark.

A dreadful, cold, cruel life it was indeed, day by day in the Diamond Palace; and at night no better. Still in the State Saloon curtseyed the mechanical ladies; in the stables the ostlers snored. — Why should they ever rouse? The great carriage-gates in the rock-crystal wall were overgrown by bindweed, and the padlocks rusted to the bars. In the Steward's Room Mandrake the Major-domo snored too. Miss Bianca, singing Patience to sleep each night with the lullaby about the doves, sometimes fancied she could hear the horrid sound even in the remoteness of the attic . . .

2

What troubled her most of all, however, as the days passed, was that the child Patience, now that she had herself, Miss Bianca, for company, seemed almost prepared to accept her dreadful lot.

"Mr. Mandrake's often told me," said Patience, "how grateful I should be . . ."

"For what?" asked Miss Bianca.

"Mr. Mandrake says, for a roof over my head," explained Patience.

"If we none of us ask more than a roof over our heads," said Miss Bianca, sharply, "lodgment in *any* prison at all must obviously be acceptable! Even in one so vulgarly diamond-studded as this!"

Patience (they were at work in the State Saloon) looked at the glittering dragon-throne, then up at the blazing chandeliers.

"Are they really vulgar?" she asked uncertainly.

"Quite odiously so," said Miss Bianca.

The child sighed.

"Do you know," she said, "sometimes I think I can remember *candles*. At least, I think they were called candles . . ."

"Did they shed a kindly light?" asked Miss Bianca.

"Oh, *yes!*" said Patience. "Especially the one by my

bed. And there was a bigger one as well — much bigger — that someone sat sewing by . . ."

"That would be a lamp," said Miss Bianca. "Lamps are kindly too."

Though she knew it was her mother Patience was trying to remember, Miss Bianca for the moment said no more, lest any further recollection should prove too distressing. But she herself recalled the kind face of the farmer's wife in the Happy Valley, and determined to lose no more time, but act at once — while Patience still remembered candles.

With or without assistance!

3

"For which I have waited too long already!" Miss Bianca chided herself. "Quite possibly by this time the Prisoners' Aid Society is rescuing someone else!" (This was truly magnanimous of her; but she always tried to believe the best of people.) "After all, Mandrake *does* unlock the back door each day, if but for a moment — and should he pursue us, at a pinch I really believe I could arouse the populace," thought Miss Bianca, "to prevent the child's recapture!"

It must be confessed that Miss Bianca had quite a clear picture of herself doing this — from some convenient point of vantage, the populace cheering below, as in photographs of Royalty coming out on balconies. But she set vanity aside, and sensibly recognized that it would be easier, if possible, to make their escape with less *éclat* — that is, when Mandrake wasn't looking.

"Think, my dear child!" said Miss Bianca to Patience. "Surely there must be *some* occasions when the back door is unlocked for something that takes longer than garbage?"

Patience thought as hard as she could.

"Last month," she said at length, "the clockmaker came. To wind up the ladies-in-waiting . . ."

"Ah!" exclaimed Miss Bianca.

"And *then* the door was left unlocked quite a long time, because he had to go back for an oilcan — and Mr. Mandrake had the Duchess's dinner to carry up, so he just left the door on the latch. If I'd only been braver!" sighed Patience.

"Never mind that now," said Miss Bianca. "A man who forgets his oilcan once will no doubt forget it again."

"I'm sure he will," agreed Patience. "Mr. Mandrake says he always forgets *something*, he's so old and absent-minded!"

"Age takes its toll," said Miss Bianca kindly. Her

spirits were rising with every word! "No doubt this good old man comes regularly?"

"Oh, yes!" said Patience.

"And when does he come next?" asked Miss Bianca.

"Next year," said Patience. "That's why Mr. Mandrake says the ladies are so wonderful: they run for a whole year . . ."

Miss Bianca's spirits sank again. A whole year! It was beyond possibility to wait a whole year. After another year, Patience might well have turned into a little automaton herself! ("And *I*," added Miss Bianca mentally, "into a *shrew!*")

She racked her brains.

"*But supposing,*" thought Miss Bianca, "*the ladies break down?*"

"If I'd only been braver!" repeated Patience sadly. "If I'd only been braver, I could have run away then!"

"Have no regrets, my dear child," said Miss Bianca briskly, "just prepare to run away tomorrow!"

4

The audacity and brilliance of Miss Bianca's plan must now of course be apparent.

Leaving Patience asleep in the attic, all through

that night Miss Bianca toiled — running from velvet skirt to velvet skirt, up by chatelaine and girdle to each velvet bodice, seeking within each steely rib-cage its center of mechanical energy. — Fortunately the Ambassador's son had a taste for clockwork; Miss Bianca, having spent more hours than she could count watching while he dismantled clockwork train or airplane or motorboat, at least knew how to *stop* clockwork. Be-

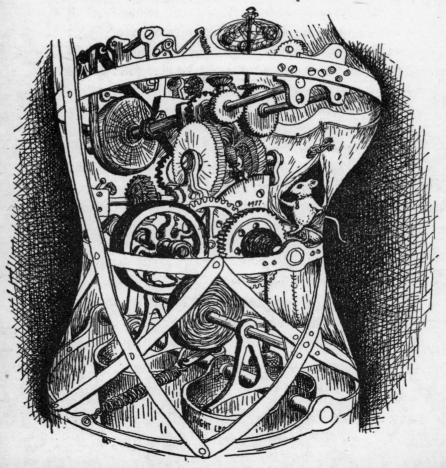

neath each velvet bodice, as she scurried down again, she left a spring loosed from its axis; as 4 A.M. struck, not a lady achieved so much as a carriage-bob, but were all collapsing where they stood!

The lady in carnation was the last to totter: as she only, in a last gasp, creaked out the inevitable formula.

"*As your Grace pleases,*" creaked the carnation lady, "*as your Grace pleases, as your Grace pleases . . .*"

Then she too ran down!

Miss Bianca stole up onto Patience's pillow, careful not to disturb the child, and composed herself for sleep. It is always wise to get a good night's rest before any important event. — Even picnics, or clambakes, or Hallowe'en parties rate an afternoon nap: how much more necessary, therefore, that Miss Bianca and Patience should sleep soundly, before a dash for freedom from a Diamond Palace.

5

Meanwhile Bernard too had been coming to a resolution.

The track on his stamp-paper carpet was by now worn quite threadbare. Half convinced as he had been by the games mistress's clever insinuations, as more and more time passed — without a word from Miss Bianca — Bernard's anxiety grew and grew. Though it might be like Miss Bianca to enjoy luxury, surely it wasn't like her to leave a whole Prisoners' Aid Society — let alone himself, thought Bernard, with rare egoism — in such suspense!

Everyone else seemed quite happy; but not Bernard. So, just like Miss Bianca, he determined to act alone, and disguised himself as a knife-grinder.

This was because (acting alone) he felt he needed to be armed to the teeth. But when he *was* — with two swords, two hatchets, three daggers and a part of a lawnmower, he couldn't move. By loading all these deadly weapons onto a little handcart, and adding a grinding wheel, he could not only get about, but would also be less conspicuous, especially since it was his humble design to approach the Diamond Palace by the back door.

He took a few lessons in knife-grinding, just in case.

Bernard said nothing of all this to the Prisoners' Aid Society. He was too much afraid of telling the members what he thought of their complacency. A flaming row, however relieving to individual feelings, does a Society nothing but harm: for instance, if any number of resignations follow, a whole useful or-

ganization may split into factions and so be rendered sterile. On the other hand, the sudden and unexplained disappearance of a Secretary can be almost equally disturbing, so before he set out conscientious Bernard mailed brief mimeographed notices all round, as follows:

> *Dear Member,*
> > *I have set out.*
> > > *Signed,*
> > > > BERNARD *(Sec.)*

9

False Hopes

Is IT REALLY to be today?" asked Patience, as soon as she woke next morning. "Is it really today that we're going to escape together?"

"To be sure it is," said Miss Bianca confidently. "Have you anything you wish to take with you?"

"Only my handkerchief," said Patience.

"The very thing," said Miss Bianca, "for you must carry me in your pocket, and I will sit on it. Meanwhile, attend the Duchess's toilet just as usual, and then we shall see what occurs at the Morning Levée — which I really think will be something quite out of the way!" said Miss Bianca.

2

Indeed it was. As the Grand Duchess emerged to receive her ladies' morning salutation, nothing met her eye but a row of collapsed velvet gowns!

"What's this?" demanded the Duchess angrily —

stirring first one, then the next, with an infuriated toe. "What's wrong with 'em, Mandrake? What's wrong with my ladies-in-waiting — ordered upon your special recommendation?"

Mandrake in turn peered at each inarticulate heap; and raised an ashen face.

"As your Grace pleases," he muttered, "they seem to need a little attention . . ."

"A little attention!" stormed the Grand Duchess, bringing her cane down across his back. "And the clockwork-maker here only last month!"

"As your Grace pleases," muttered Mandrake, "perhaps I should summon him again . . ."

"Summon him this very instant!" screamed the Duchess.

How the hearts of Patience and Miss Bianca lifted! — Patience's hand, in her apron pocket, almost squeezed the breath out of Miss Bianca's body, in delighted congratulations. For of course she realized at once that this was somehow all Miss Bianca's doing. Bending her head down to whisper —

"We'll run away as soon as the door's open, won't we, Miss Bianca?" whispered Patience eagerly.

"Indeed we will!" Miss Bianca whispered back. "Poor Mandrake! I could almost feel it in my heart to pity him!"

But they reckoned without the Duchess's imperious nature.

"Only first call my coach!" screamed the Duchess.

"Your — your Grace's coach?" repeated Mandrake, stammering with astonishment.

"To carry me to my hunting lodge!" screamed the Duchess. "If I can't be properly waited on in my Diamond Palace, you and the child shall wait upon me in my hunting lodge!"

Even as she spoke her gaunt right hand, weighted with diamond rings, descended on Patience's shoulder. The big knuckles ground cruelly against Patience's collarbone, the long fingers, strong as an eagle's talons, almost met in the child's emaciated, shrinking flesh; Patience stood as helpless as if she'd been turned to stone.

And never once did that terrible grip loosen, all the time Mandrake, in the stables, roused the astonished ostlers, and bade them harness the no less astonished horses, and then set them with hammer and wedge to force open the great gates in the rock-crystal wall. — Not only the back door, but the great gates were to be opened! Even up in the State Saloon, Patience and Miss Bianca could hear quite plainly first the thumping, then the clanging, then the grinding over gravel, interspersed with wicked language whenever

an ostler hit his thumb. But they were powerless to take advantage. The Duchess held Patience as in a vise; and sounds which should have been music to their ears but deepened their despair!

"Ask if you should not prepare her baggage!" whispered Miss Bianca desperately.

"Please, your Grace, don't you want me to prepare your baggage?" gasped Patience.

"My Grace will find everything needful where she's going!" snapped the Duchess. "Stand still, child!"

"Her jewels, then!" prompted Miss Bianca — in whose experience no great lady ever traveled without her jewel box. "Ask if you may not fetch her jewel box!"

"Mayn't I even fetch your Grace's jewel box?" gasped Patience.

"I shall find jewels too!" snarled the Duchess. "And canes too, and whips too! Stand as I bid you!"

She never let go Patience's shoulder until she had pushed the child before her into the great, dirty, dilapidated coach. All the stuffing was coming out of the seats, cats had littered on the floor; for a moment, as the Duchess climbed in, it seemed as though the very springs would give, under her wicked weight. But though the whole vehicle sagged lopsidedly, it somehow held together. — Then Mandrake bolted

them in, and mounted the box, and whipped up the horses . . .

It was at this moment that Bernard, with his knife-grinder's cart, appeared making for the back door.

It stood wide open. Mandrake, so harried and hustled, had dispatched to the clockwork-maker not only a message, but a key. The message included strict injunctions not to leave the door unlocked, still less ajar even, for a single instant; but this time the clockwork-maker had forgotten his screwdriver, and really he was too old to bother.

So Bernard, his handcart with him, entered the Diamond Palace without the least difficulty or delay.

Only of course he didn't find Miss Bianca. He was just five minutes too late.

10

A Coach Ride

MISS BIANCA HADN'T seen him; but Patience had.

"Did you see that mouse with the little cart?" asked Patience cautiously. (Some few miles later, when the Duchess's great dirty wig began to nod.)

"I was in your pocket, child," said Miss Bianca. "I saw nothing."

"Well, there *was* one," said Patience. "Do you think it could have been Bernard?"

Miss Bianca shook her head hopelessly. She was in dreadfully low spirits. And no wonder: so nearly had her plan succeeded, and it was such a clever plan, bitter it was indeed to be cheated of the fruits! Moreover, there was no telling but that their future situation might be even worse than that they left behind: at least in the Diamond Palace there had been twelve ladies for the Duchess to abuse, whereas at the hunting lodge the full brunt of her temper would have to be borne by Patience and Mandrake — the child no doubt bearing the worst of it!

"Don't you think," persisted Patience, "we should throw out some sort of *clue*, just in case? Shall I throw out my handkerchief? Or suppose you threw out your silver chain?"

Miss Bianca flinched. At that moment of utter despondency her silver chain seemed her one remaining link with the happy past. It was a gift from the Boy's mother, fully an inch long and of the most exquisite workmanship, and it had never been off Miss Bianca's neck since she received it. She had worn it even in the Black Castle; each time she fingered it, what beautiful memories came flooding back! — of her Porcelain Pagoda, with its swansdown cushions; of Ambassadorial dinner parties, when it was so much admired; best of all, of the Boy himself, her kind protector and playmate . . . "I should never have let them make me Madam Chairwoman at all," thought Miss Bianca sadly, "if I am to be reft perpetually from his side! And am I now to sacrifice my precious silver chain — my last memento of him — just *in case?*"

She sighed again. So did Patience.

"It's the only one I've got," sighed Patience, as she

gently took her handkerchief out from underneath Miss Bianca and screwed it into a ball.

Miss Bianca looked at the grimy, crumpled scrap of cotton. If crumpled and grimy, it was because Patience had so often cried into it: the little blood spots showed where Patience had pricked her fingers on the diamond stars of the Duchess's wig . . .

"I'm afraid you won't be so comfortable, in my pocket, without it," apologized Patience.

"I should be ashamed of myself!" thought Miss Bianca — and with one swift gesture unclasped the clasp and threw her precious chain out of the coach window.

As soon as she had done so, she felt much better. It was the fact that nothing made Miss Bianca feel so low — not even hopes disappointed, nor fears for the future — as being selfish. Children know this feeling too, which was probably why Patience, prepared to give up her one-and-only handkerchief, had been able to encourage and support Miss Bianca instead of the other way round.

And in fact the idea of throwing out a clue, just in case, proved to be a very sensible and valuable one. Bernard *found* it!

2

Bernard wasn't a particularly clever mouse, but any involvement with Miss Bianca preternaturally sharpened his wits. Thus, discovering the Diamond Palace deserted, he immediately concluded that its occupants must have *gone* somewhere; also, probably by some means of transport. This notion led him back to the great gates to examine the gravel for hoof or wheel tracks. Discovering both —

"A coach!" thought Bernard.

Examining the tracks a bit further on —

"Bound outwards from the city!" he thought.

And then, with a really splendid feat of memory —

"Also a certain hunting lodge," recalled Bernard, from the speech he had made about the Grand Duchess at the General Meeting, *"situated in the forest"* — this was the bit he had been going to say when the Professor of Mathematics interrupted him — *"above the Happy Valley . . ."*

So at least he knew which direction to follow, even when the wheel tracks were obliterated by the marks of bicycle or motor tires. Sometimes pushing his handcart before him, sometimes pulling it behind, off in pursuit hurried Bernard as fast as he could.

All the same, the Duchess's coach was already some

miles ahead, and fast as Bernard hurried he was no
match for two coach-horses, however aged. He grew
hotter and hotter, and tireder and tireder, and the
hatchets rattled about in his handcart, and the part of
a lawnmower kept falling off, so that the finding of
Miss Bianca's silver chain was just what was needed
to put fresh heart into him.

What a mercy it hadn't been found first by gipsies!

It would have made a gipsy-daughter's wédding-dowry. But there it lay still inviolate, glittering like frost upon the bramblebush that had received it.

Bernard pressed it to his whiskers. He wouldn't have done so if there was anyone looking. Mice, for all their interracial connections, remain less Latin than Anglo-Saxon when it comes to any display of emotion. But since no one *was* looking, Bernard pressed it to his whiskers . . .

And now, just as though the chain possessed some white magic of its own, a lorry first overhauled him (having nearly over*run* him), then halted while the driver and his mate ate lunch. In large letters over the cab, FOREST AND HAPPY VALLEY PIT-PROP CO. read Bernard. He instantly made fast his cart to a trailing rope, and himself scrambled up over a rear wheel.

Once in motion again, they actually *overtook* the Duchess's coach. The lorry was well into the forest before Mandrake whipped his horses along the first broad ride between the first tall trees.

Then it broke down.

3

"Did you see that lorry?" asked Patience of Miss Bianca.

"No, child," said Miss Bianca — speaking now more cheerfully, but without any particular interest. "Remember that I am in your pocket."

"I might have called out," sighed Patience, "but we passed by before I thought of it . . ."

If only she *had* called out! — If only *Miss Bianca* had called out! The sound of that beloved voice would have spurred Bernard to nip driver and mate from their tea-making (they always made tea when the lorry broke down) and make them stop the coach (as probably containing some important person) to complain of the awful hazards their Union rules subjected them to, such as being mouse-nipped on the road. If this had happened Patience and Miss Bianca would have been rescued at once, lorry-drivers having in general very good hearts.

But Patience didn't call out; and on the coach rolled; and not until half-an-hour later did Bernard, fidgeting about while the kettle boiled for a second brew, recognize its wheel tracks; when in a desperation of impatience, as the driver and his mate began to make French toast, he unhitched his handcart and followed after — once more alone.

11

The Hunting Lodge

AT LAST THE coach halted. The last few miles of
forest had been so dense, branches rattled on its roof:
the clearing in which stood the Duchess's hunting
lodge was no bigger than a tennis court: the building
itself so closely hemmed by trees, they must have
doubly darkened windows already half-blind with
unclipped ivy. The Duchess's hunting lodge was as
dark as her Diamond Palace had been bright . . .

Patience shivered; and Miss Bianca with her.

For welcome, out bounded two huge bloodhounds,
fawning about the Duchess's feet.

"Down, Tyrant! Down, Torment!" she cried. — Yet
their very names seemed to give her pleasure. She
repeated them almost lovingly. "Brave Torment, brave
Tyrant!" she cried. "Have you been too long without
proper duties, that you slaver so? I put you upon
duty again! — Where's your master?" she added.
"Where's my Chief Ranger?"

Up behind the bloodhounds loomed a figure almost grimmer than Mandrake's — bearded like a pard, strong long legs booted to the knee, enormous hands gauntleted to the elbows, and one of them clutching an iron cudgel!

"I put *you* upon duty too!" cried the Grand Duchess.

2

Much as she had hated the Diamond Palace, Miss Bianca instantly hated the hunting lodge far more. If the Palace's diamond-studded vulgarity had often made her feel positive nausea, the hunting lodge, in all its plainness, Miss Bianca immediately knew was going to make her feel something even worse. She didn't give this emotion an exact name; but it was fear.

Patience wasn't to have an attic, in the hunting lodge, but a little cellar; or cell. Mandrake directed her to it at once, with instructions to stay there until sent for to undress the Duchess. "As you will stay there accordingly," ordered Mandrake, "whenever off duty!"

Between its narrow, damp, dark walls Patience and Miss Bianca looked at each other — each striving to conceal from the other that unnamed emotion.

"I suppose I shall spend *some* time upstairs?" said Patience bravely.

"To be sure you will!" replied Miss Bianca.

She gently rubbed Patience's shoulder where the Duchess's grip had bruised it.

"I wonder what the Duchess meant," said Patience presently, "about putting those dreadful great dogs *on duty?*"

Miss Bianca wondered too.

"Are they police-dogs, do you think?" asked Patience. "To prevent anyone trying to escape?"

Hitherto, such was the child's true affection for her only friend, the idea of escaping had never been mentioned since they were forced from the Diamond Palace into the Duchess's coach. Far from reproaching Miss Bianca with fruitlessly raising her hopes, Patience so suffered for Miss Bianca's disappointment, she immediately attempted a sort of apology for even using the word.

"I meant, to prevent anyone just going for a walk in the forest," explained Patience.

Just then, both Mandrake and the Grand Duchess shouted for her at once. Off poor Patience ran — leaving Miss Bianca, touched almost to tears, to rack her brains again as she had racked them in the Diamond Palace . . .

3

"It is evidently Tyrant and Torment we have to fear most," thought Miss Bianca. (She knew quite well that by *going for a walk in the forest* Patience meant *running away through the forest*.) "Without *them* on the scent, even the Chief Ranger, big and grim as he is, might well be at a loss. If only we could but win them to take our part!" thought Miss Bianca.

"Appearances may deceive," mused Miss Bianca. "We cannot all be born beautiful; beneath many a rugged exterior beats a kind heart; perhaps Tyrant and Torment are less bloodthirsty than they naturally (being bloodhounds) are forced to look. Who knows but what our predicament, put to them in a few simple words, may not even touch their hearts? I think I'll pay them a little visit."

If Bernard had been there (in fact he was still plunging about the forest), he would have of course tried to stop her, on the grounds that she would instantly be eaten up. But Bernard wasn't there, and actually Miss Bianca's confidence proved fully justified. There was ever the air about her, however modestly she bore herself, of a V.I.P. (or Very Important Person) such as police forces, far from consuming, turn out guards of honor for. As Miss Bianca

entered Tyrant's and Torment's quarters, both bloodhounds rose smartly to their feet and saluted!

"Pray forgive me if I intrude," said Miss Bianca,
bowing back with easy grace, "but I just happened to
be passing; and dropped in for a little chat."

"Always honored to see a lady in Mess," replied
Sergeant Tyrant readily. "Corporal Torment, find her
a seat!"

While Corporal Torment looked about for something Miss Bianca's size, Miss Bianca too looked about,
despite all her anxieties, with unaffected interest.
She had never been in police quarters before. Even
among military men she knew only Lancers and Hus-
sars — with whom, after they'd jingled alongside the
Ambassador's carriage, she and the Boy occasionally
lunched. Here was certainly no glittering Regimental
plate — no shelf of cups won at polo or cricket; but a
well-scrubbed decency reigned, and she had no hesita-
tion in sitting down when at last Corporal Torment
produced what appeared to be a particularly well-
scrubbed ivory bench. — "Whatever else I do,"
thought Miss Bianca, "I must *not* look like the Colo-
nel's wife visiting Married Quarters!" — and so
didn't examine her seat too closely, but instead
launched out into light chat.

"What an agreeable *dépôt* this must seem to you,"

began Miss Bianca, "if you, like myself, are lovers of our famous forests? Such beauty of trees, and undergrowth! What very happy bloodhounds you must be, stationed in such exquisite, afforested surroundings!"

It will be seen that she wasn't using particularly simple words just yet, but most troops like being talked to a bit over their heads, and Tyrant and Torment were no exception. Their big ears wagged appreciatively as they listened, receptive to whatever the lady had to say. Only they neither of them said anything back, and as Miss Bianca wasn't there merely to give them pleasure, or even to teach them appreciation of natural beauty, after a few more well-turned phrases she *did* simplify.

"The dawn glimpsed through birch trees," exclaimed Miss Bianca, "what rare delights! What chiaroscuro! — I'm sure you both write to your mothers about it frequently."

Though they still didn't speak, she thought they certainly looked touched!

"Or if either of you has a little sister," continued Miss Bianca, much encouraged, "perhaps you write to *her?* — Possibly you have observed," she added lightly, "*someone's* little sister just come into residence here at this moment?"

At last Tyrant spoke again.

"Blue eyes, fair hair, height about four foot, weight about sixty pounds: description already circulated," agreed Sergeant Tyrant.

4

Miss Bianca was so shocked, it took even her a few moments to recover poise, as she suddenly realized that some appearances evidently did *not* deceive! Those few heartlessly professional words revealed Tyrant a police officer to the marrow, immune to every softer feeling. It was his mournful, touched gaze that had deceived — probably just due to the way his eyelids drooped — not the cruel set of his jaw! Probably he never wrote to his mother at all.

"Why, you make the poor child sound like a criminal!" cried Miss Bianca indignantly.

"Juvenile delinquent," corrected Tyrant.

"Such as is our duty to pursue," put in Torment, "with the full rigor of the Law."

"But *Patience* isn't a delinquent!" cried Miss Bianca. "She has never done anything wrong in her life!"

"But she *might*," pointed out Tyrant.

"Such as running away," added Torment. "They *do*, don't they, Sarge?"

116

Miss Bianca shuddered. But with a great effort she managed to conceal her true emotions.

"Naturally it is your function to pursue," she agreed. "And when giving chase to escaping murderers, for instance, your selfless devotion must be the admiration of all. I'm sure *I* admire the police-force quite enormously. But such a mite as Patience — only sixty pounds, remember! — is surely beneath your notice? Really, you'd look quite ridiculous — two such great bloodhounds as you are! If *Patience* went running through the forest, surely you wouldn't pursue *her?*" pressed Miss Bianca.

Sergeant Tyrant and Corporal Torment wrinkled their brows. — All bloodhounds' brows are perpetually wrinkled, because they are such slow thinkers. They never think a single thought their fathers and grandfathers haven't thought before them; and even so have to remember, and ruminate, and check up. But when they have done all this, they are as stubborn as only the stupid can be.

"If so ordered, we would," said Tyrant.

"By her Grace," added Torment.

"Seeing as it's her Grace's orders we're under," explained Tyrant.

It was just at this moment that Miss Bianca, as she lowered her eyes to conceal the contempt and repugnance in them, perceived precisely what it was she was sitting on. Her artistic studies had of course included Anatomy: what she was sitting on was a very small shinbone — gnawed.

"But she'll be too tired to run tonight — eh, Sarge?" grinned Corporal Torment.

5

"My dear child," exclaimed Miss Bianca, as soon as Patience returned from putting the Duchess's wig away, "we must flee this very evening! It is our only hope — if Tyrant and Torment are not to pursue us and probably tear us into pieces!"

"Oh, dear," sighed Patience, "I'm so tired already — and my shoulder still aches so!"

" 'Tis our only hope!" repeated Miss Bianca vigorously. "Also I have looked at the map in the hall —" (she had found it on her way back from Tyrant's and Torment's quarters) "— and discovered that we are no more than a league north from the Happy Valley! Once there, I promise you will never have to run anywhere again! Pluck up your courage, my dear child, put me in your pocket, and let us both make a last bid, however bold, for freedom and happiness!"

Tired as she was — her shoulder still aching — at

these words of Miss Bianca's Patience *did* pluck up courage!

6

At least the Duchess's hunting lodge wasn't nearly so well bolted and barred as her Diamond Palace. Or perhaps Mandrake was too exhausted after the journey to go round properly. In any case, there was a little window left half open on the ground floor. Patience needed only a very small space to squeeze through! — and lost only her handkerchief in the process.

Once outside they paused a moment, listening. All was still. They looked back at the high gloomy bulk of the lodge: not a light showed.

"Hold me up, child," said Miss Bianca, "so that I can see the stars!"

Patience held Miss Bianca up on her palm. Miss Bianca scrutinized the heavens. She recognized the Great Bear at once — his tail pointing to the north. "The Happy Valley lying to the south, we leave your honorable tail behind us, do we not, honored Ursus Major?" cried Miss Bianca. — She was so well-educated, she knew all the proper forms of address; and indeed the Great Bear, pleased at being given his classic name, seemed to shine all the brighter. "Quite right, you little atomy!" growled the Great Bear kindly. (In a charcoal-burner's hut in the forest it sounded like a clap of thunder.) "Off, away with you, and leave *me* to my duty of holding true the North Star!"

"So we must leave the North Star behind us," said Miss Bianca to Patience. "Can you remember?"

"I'll try to!" said Patience bravely — even though she shivered a little in the cold night air.

There was a wide opening in the very direction they needed to follow. Tucking Miss Bianca back into her pocket, Patience stole softly into its shade. Underfoot she felt moss and beechmast — so easy to run on, soon, as her eyes grew accustomed to the darkness, she was running quite fast, yet so smoothly that Miss Bianca felt the motion almost agreeable. "This is better than one could have dared anticipate!" thought Miss Bianca. "How right we were, to seize our opportunity!"

Though the air was cold, it was also sweet — with the breath of freedom!

7

But by what mischance, in the hunting lodge behind them, did the Duchess suddenly wake?

As a rule she slept heavily all through the night. She didn't even dream, for she had nothing to dream about. All she desired — wealth, and power, and especially the power to give pain — was hers to enjoy by day. Possibly it was the unaccustomed bed; but for whatever reason, the Grand Duchess suddenly woke — and when Mandrake came running at the furious peal of her bell, demanded the child Patience!

"Send me the child Patience," ordered the Duchess, "to come and rub my feet!"

Off shambled Mandrake in his dressing-gown and slippers — losing first the right-foot slipper, then the left, in his haste to do his mistress's bidding. After a thorough search of the hunting lodge, however, he returned at a slower pace . . .

"As your Grace pleases," mumbled Mandrake nervously, "the child doesn't seem to be about . . ."

"Not *about?*" shouted the Duchess. "If she's asleep, wake her up! What d'you mean, *not about?*"

"As your Grace pleases — not here," mumbled the Major-domo. "That is, nowhere to be found . . ."

Perhaps the worst thing of all was that the Duchess had faced the same situation before. As the little shin-bone bore witness.

"What, run off already?" screamed the Duchess. "Rouse my Chief Ranger!" she screamed. "Loose Tyrant and Torment! Bring her back, if not alive, then dead!"

Instantly all was bustle and confusion. — Bustle not unpurposeful, however, nor confusion undirected! Out to the Chief Ranger's quarters stumbled Mandrake, back they both hastened to unleash the bloodhounds. Patience's handkerchief (found caught on the window sash) was presented to their noses. Tyrant and Torment recognized upon it also a trace of mouse-scent. "Easy meat, Sarge!" bayed Corporal Torment. — It was so long since they had been let loose, they bounded forth absolutely slavering with anticipation. The Chief Ranger seized his cudgel and followed, as they galloped into the forest while the Duchess shrieked a view-halloo from her bedroomwindow. "View-halloo!" shrieked the Duchess. "Viewhalloo, good Tyrant and Torment! Bring back your meat alive or dead!"

8

"Do you know," said Miss Bianca to Patience, as they paused for a brief moment, "though I wouldn't wish to alarm you, it does seem as though I just heard something that sounded *rather* like the voice of Torment."

They were in the very thick of the forest. Beneath

the close-growing trees an undergrowth of brambles sprawled their thorny trails across a path no longer mossy but strewn with biggish stones. Patience had once or twice been tripped up by them.

"I thought *I* heard it too," said Patience nervously.

"Then do you think you could run a little faster?" suggested Miss Bianca.

"I'll *try*," said Patience.

Of course Bernard was in the forest with them; but his handcart having bogged down against a giant mushroom, he was completely occupied in extricating it . . .

12

Bloodhounds in the Forest

IT WAS A long, dreadful night indeed, to Patience and Miss Bianca — running and running, pausing just for a moment when Patience had a stitch, then running and running again! — In the thick of the forest as they now were, they had certain advantages: so many rabbit and ferret runs, so many fox and badger paths, confused their scent. But it *was* Torment Miss Bianca had heard: fleeter of foot than his sergeant (as corporals often are), Torment had at once taken the lead, and well it was for Patience and Miss Bianca that his nose now and then betrayed him!

On and on they ran. Their only respite was in the hut of a charcoal-burner. The great forests above the Happy Valley were full of such; fortunately the fugitives happened upon one not only hospitable but honest. Its lighted window might have lured them both but to disaster — many of the charcoal-burners doubling their humble profession with that of jackals to the Chief Ranger, whom they helped to lay not a few poor poachers by the heels. And even here, after Patience had been given a cup of milk, and Miss Bianca a morsel of cheese, and both had been let sit an hour by the fire, it was plain that they weren't exactly welcome . . .

"I ask no questions," said the honest charcoal-burner, "nor no questions will I answer neither — to whomsoever be pursuing of ye! All the same — hearing her Grace's Chief Ranger's whistle — let alone the baying of her Grace's bloodhounds — also seeing as I'm a man wi' wife and childer —"

Patience looked wistfully at the warm hearth. But already contact with Miss Bianca had taught her true courtesy.

"Then I'll just run on again," said Patience politely, "and thank you very much for the milk."

2

"I'd almost rather they brought her back alive, mused the Duchess to Mandrake, as he obsequiously served her a horrible snack of warmed-up jugged hare.

"Your Grace's tender heart is well known," said Mandrake.

But even he, cruel as he was, shuddered to think of

the fate of the child Patience if the Chief Ranger *did* bring her back alive . . .

3

Every bramble-trail of the undergrowth tore at Patience's skirt and clawed her ankles, the lower branches of young saplings lashed her eyes, big roots tripped her up. If her fingers had bled from the diamond stars in the Duchess's wig, her poor legs now bled even worse, from thorn and bramble. Painful as was the sting of the Duchess's cane, much more so the whip of a hazel-wand! Yet on and on Patience ran — Miss Bianca in her pocket — as brave a little girl as ever lived.

Whenever she had to stop, Miss Bianca encouraged her in the coolest way.

"I was particularly pleased by your nice manners, dear child," panted Miss Bianca (actually feeling quite faint herself from so much bumping about). "You spoke very nicely indeed to that poor but honest charcoal-burner."

"Did I?" gasped Patience. "I wanted so much to stay!"

"Which makes it all the more creditable," said Miss Bianca. "Anyone can be polite in a drawing room, but to be polite while fleeing from bloodhounds shows a truly educated heart. — Now, can that be Tyrant's voice I hear as well? Perhaps you'd better run on."

On Patience ran again. After Miss Bianca's praise the trees seemed less thick, and the brambles less prickly, and she didn't stumble quite so often. Soon she was running downhill. With surprising sudden-ness the forest thinned and dwindled — first to mere scrub, then to a mere hedgerow bordering a sunken road. They were reaching the Valley at last! — and there, just where the road bent, stood one enormous oak . . .

Miss Bianca recognized it instantly.

"Just as far as the next turning," she cried, "and up the path beyond! Run, my dear Patience, run — for it really *is* Tyrant's voice!"

With a last effort Patience ran so fast that Miss Bianca was almost thrown out. She had to hold on to the inside of the pocket with both hands.

"We've come to a house!" gasped Patience.

"And safety!" panted Miss Bianca. "Ring the bell!"

"I can't reach it!" sobbed Patience.

"Then knock!" panted Miss Bianca. "Both Tyrant *and* Torment I hear! Knock louder!"

"I'm knocking as hard as I can!" sobbed Patience.

At that moment, the bloodhounds rounded the

corner by the oak tree — heads down, jaws drooling, eyes aflame. Why, oh *why* didn't the door open!

4

Inside, in the big comfortable kitchen, the farmer stood up and yawned.

"Time for bed, wife," said he.

"Aye, time for bed," said she.

She put out the two big lamps while her husband kicked apart the fire. A last flicker of light chased the shadows across the ceiling; the scarlet geraniums showed velvety-black against the warm, comfortable curtains.

"Seeing as I'll be up at five," said the farmer, "and the boys no later, for all they're still out dancing, the gay gallivants!"

"Gay gallivants, gay workers," said his wife. "There'll be hot porridge ready for ye. — But listen, husband, to the dogs' cry!"

"After a poacher," said the farmer, "that's all."

" 'Send he gets back safe to his littl'uns!" said the farmer's wife.

They neither of them heard Patience beating at the door. The big iron knocker was so heavy, and her hands were so small, and she was so exhausted, she wasn't making very much noise, and what she did the baying of the bloodhounds drowned.

"God bless this house," said the farmwife, "and all poor homeless ones abroad!" Then she and her husband went to bed.

5

"I don't think they're *going* to open!" sobbed Patience.

Miss Bianca glanced hastily back. For an instant the bloodhounds' pace was slower — they were alongside the pigsties; it was a moment's respite — but only a moment's. The thought of what might happen in *another* moment, absolutely there on the doorstep, so near to sanctuary yet so hopeless to achieve it, froze Miss Bianca's blood.

"At least we can't stay *here*," she gasped, "to be pulled in pieces! Run on again, child!"

"I can't!" sobbed Patience. "I'm too tired!"

It was a time for desperate measures. Miss Bianca did a thing she'd never done in her life. Baring her small white teeth, customarily employed on nothing tougher than cream cheese, right through apron and frock and petticoat she gave Patience a sharp nip.

"*Now* will you run!" ordered Miss Bianca. "If we

may but reach the dovecote — across that vegetable patch to the right — there is yet hope!"

Patience ran.

6

Fortunate that Miss Bianca's preliminary investigation of the farm had been so thorough! — otherwise she wouldn't have known about the dovecote at all. As it was, she remembered not only its situation, but also that there was a ladder inside leading up to a broad ledge below the first tier of nesting boxes. That bloodhounds cannot climb ladders is of course common knowledge, but it was Miss Bianca's conscientiousness in the first place that enabled her to profit by it.

"Now up the ladder!" ordered Miss Bianca — regretfully but sensibly nipping Patience again; and as they at last reached precarious, temporary safety, drew her first full breath for what seemed like years . . .

7

All around them the doves woke up and began to coo.

"Who's here, who, who?" cooed the doves. "Do *you* know who, my doo?" "Two, two!" cooed the doves nesting nearest. "But we don't know *who!*"

Since Patience obviously couldn't tell them, also it was obviously necessary that they should be reassured, how fortunate, again, that Miss Bianca was a perfect mistress of their language! — which she had studied in the course of singing-lessons.

"Pray forgive the intrusion," called up Miss Bianca

— pitching her voice with all the accuracy of a prima donna, and with a much better accent than most prima donnas have, in a foreign tongue — "and allow myself and my young friend to beg your hospitality! We are neither rogues and vagabonds nor fugitives from justice: there just happen to be a couple of bloodhounds following us."

"Who, who did you say?" cooed the doves interestedly.

But Miss Bianca felt it quite beyond her to explain the nature of bloodhounds to sleepy doves — who are stupid enough even when wide awake!

"Large birds," said Miss Bianca. "But they will not enter here, being afraid of enclosed spaces." ("True, true!" cooed the doves, not wishing to seem ignorant.) "Therefore, with your permission," continued Miss Bianca, "we will occupy this very commodious ledge until morning, and then be on our way — leaving you to the happy knowledge of a charitable act gracefully performed."

Miss Bianca's eloquence rarely failed of effect, nor did it now. Even though the doves understood few of the big words, they felt reassured and flattered, and after a few consenting coos all went back to sleep.

"Are these the doves you sang to me about?" asked

Patience, as she and Miss Bianca settled themselves on the ledge.

"No, indeed!" said Miss Bianca, rather sharply. "*They* had sense! — Now we have but to hold out till morning," she added cheerfully, "and help will surely come. Oh my dear child, what loving arms will then receive you!"

"I'm sure I'll try to hold out," said Patience. "I'm only afraid of falling off this ledge. — Will loving arms *really* receive me," she asked wistfully, "if the bloodhounds don't first?"

"You may take my word for it," said Miss Bianca bravely.

But morning was still many hours off; and the Duchess's Chief Ranger, who *could* climb ladders, was certainly following behind his hounds . . .

Miss Bianca hoped Patience had forgotten the Chief Ranger. She almost wished she could forget him herself!

"Where, oh *where*," thought Miss Bianca desperately, "is Bernard?"

13

The Last Stand

ONLY HIS FAITHFUL handcart kept him on his
legs. Wearily poor Bernard struggled on, leaning on its
shafts: when he came to a dip, and the cart could roll
downhill, he even snatched a brief ride on them, otherwise he might have collapsed altogether. By this time
he had lost all sense of direction, he was just keeping
on; and it was by the merest chance that he stumbled
into a little track beaten through the undergrowth
where the going was easier.

At the end of the track stood a charcoal-burner's hut.

Bernard stopped outside simply because he *had* to
stop somewhere. He didn't knock at the door. Only
because the charcoal-burner was just setting out to do
a little poaching on his own account, and saw him, did
Bernard speak up — to show he wasn't a burglar.

"Any knives to grind?" asked Bernard hopelessly.

"Nary a one," said the charcoal-burner.

"No scissors of your wife's?" suggested Bernard automatically.

"No scissors neither," said the charcoal-burner, "to the best of my belief." — He looked at Bernard shrewdly: even the disguise of a knife-grinder, and after all his dusty travels, couldn't conceal Bernard's inherent respectability. "But since you're such a decent-looking sort of mouse, I'll ask."

"Don't bother," said Bernard.

But the charcoal-burner was already calling over his shoulder.

"Martha!" he shouted. "Any scissors to grind?"

"What, at this time of night?" called back his wife inside the hut. "Whatever makes you ask?"

"Just because here's a decent-looking mouse willing to grind 'em!" called the charcoal-burner.

At that, his wife came out to see. She too gave Bernard a good look, and shook her head regretfully.

"Neither scissors nor skewers," said she. "But I must say mice seem to be mending their ways! For let alone here's one earning an honest livelihood, that little white lady in the child's pocket had the prettiest manners ever seen!"

Bernard was up in a flash. All his weariness was cast aside like a mackintosh when the sun comes out.

"When were they here?" he asked eagerly.

"Why, this same night as ever is!" said the charcoal-burner's wife. "They left not an hour ago!"

"Which way?" gasped Bernard.

"Since there be only one track through the forest at all passable," said the charcoal-burner, "you'll have no difficulty in following 'em!"

With but the briefest word of thanks — barely remembering the civility of a pull at his whiskers — Bernard seized his handcart and rushed off in the direction indicated.

He was but a mile behind Patience and Miss Bianca in the dovecote — but Torment and Tyrant, to say nothing of the Chief Ranger, were still *between* them!

2

The reason the Chief Ranger wasn't already up with his bloodhounds was that, like every other wicked person, he feared the brave farmers of the Happy Valley. They turned angry, contemptuous faces upon him even when he was hunting poachers; if they had guessed he was hunting a child — and a girl-child! — they'd have ducked him at least, if not tarred and feathered him. With his long booted legs he should have overtaken Patience in the forest itself — and indeed only the accident of her finding refuge in the charcoal-burner's hut had saved her. But when he perceived, upon examining her fresh tracks, that she had actually gained the Happy Valley, he held back, waiting till dead of night (when all the brave farmers would be asleep), and trusting to his bloodhounds to find and hold the quarry. He knew that at his whistle and call of "Come, Tyrant! Stay, Torment!" the one would rush bounding to fetch him while the other remained on guard.

So exactly it happened, when he at last reached the sunken road. — Shrill blew his whistle, carryingly echoed his voice; within a matter of seconds Tyrant slavered beside him under the oak tree. "What, no blood on thy jaws?" joked the Chief Ranger grimly. "Has one small maid been too much for 'ee? Ah, well, so maybe her Grace'll like it better to have her back alive!"

Then he followed Tyrant along the path to the dovecote.

One hardly knows whether it is a point in his favor or not that he'd have preferred to find the *remains*. The Chief Ranger himself thought it a great point, as showing he was such a kindly-natured sort of chap he'd much rather all was over before he got there. The pleas of poachers, regarding their wives and children, he used to say often quite upset him, as he broke their wrists with his cudgel and set his dogs a-tearing of their raiment. He was nonetheless prepared — duty being duty, especially with a pension in sight — to fling Patience over his shoulder and carry her back into servitude with the Grand Duchess.

Outside the dovecote lay Torment on guard.

"What, no blood on *thy* jaws either?" joked the Chief Ranger. "All work left to yours truly? Well, well! Why didn't ye go in after?"

"Ladder, ladder, ladder!" bayed Torment.

"Oh, so she's up a ladder, is she?" said the Chief Ranger — and pushed his big bearded face, grinningly, through the dovecote door . . .

3

Miss Bianca and Patience were still not quite so defenseless as they seemed — or at least Miss Bianca wasn't. Every word of this colloquy had been overheard by her, and as her ears were sharp, so were her wits keen. However exhausted, first by natural fatigue, then by watching (fearful lest Patience, who *was* asleep, should fall off the ledge), Miss Bianca still kept her wits, and perceived one last useful stratagem.

"Wake the doves again!" cried Miss Bianca. "Fire! Rats! Hawks!" she shrieked — conjuring up every peril most feared by their hosts. "Oh wake the doves," cried Miss Bianca, "till they wake the house! Call and scream, child, as loud as you can!"

As the big bearded face pushed through the door —

"Fire! Rats! Hawks!" cried Patience.

"Hawks! Rats! Fire!" shrilled Miss Bianca.

"Rats! Fire! Hawks!" cried both together.

All the doves woke up at once, and without knowing precisely what was going on, took up the cry.

4

"Listen, husband! Seems as though there be something disturbable to my dovecote," said the farmer's wife. "I trust no rat's found entry!"

"Doves be so foolish, they'll wake and create at a shadow," said the farmer sleepily. "I'll still take a look in the morning, just to please 'ee . . ."

"What if morning's too late?" asked his wife.

"Five o'clock's early enough for any man," grumbled the farmer, sinking his big heavy head back into the big feather-pillow.

His wife was too good a wife to argue. She just sat

up a moment longer, hoping there was nothing really amiss in her dovecote, and then pulled her nightcap back over her ears and went to sleep too.

5

A flurry of blue-gray wings swirled down about the Chief Ranger's head; for a moment he was almost blinded by them, as the hubbub almost deafened him. The doves — at least a hundred of them — could have pecked his eyes out! But unfortunately they had no imagination: the Chief Ranger didn't look like any large bird, such as Miss Bianca had told them of; no hawk was in sight, and the cry of "Rats!" or "Fire!" being a favorite practical joke with their own teen-agers, within a matter of seconds each foolish dove had returned to its perch.

Reassured by the sudden calm, the Chief Ranger set his foot upon the ladder.

How easy, now, before dawn broke, before the brave farmers of the Happy Valley were awake, to throw a child over his shoulder and carry her off!

The ladder creaked beneath his weight as he began to climb . . .

"Oh *where*," thought Miss Bianca again, desperately — *it might be for the last time* — "is Bernard?"

6

He was at the dovecote door! — Having followed the right direction at a speed perfectly incredible!

The rumor of the frightened doves reached him just as he entered the farmyard; leaning on the shafts of his handcart he covered the intervening ground like a racing motorist. Crash went the handcart against the door sill — he dragged it across! "Bernard!" shrieked Miss Bianca — one upward glance, and he took in the whole appalling situation!

"Cut down the ladder!" shrieked Miss Bianca.

Bernard seized a hatchet off the handcart. How he wished he had four arms instead of two, to hew with both his hatchets at once! Even that would have taken too long, for the wood was hickory, the hardest wood there is. — Bernard snatched up a sword, and put himself in a posture to attack. But though he had taken lessons in knife-grinding, he had inexplicably omitted to take lessons in swordsmanship: the first flourish of the unaccustomed weapon nearly lopped his own ears off. Bernard flung it aside with a groan — hatchets and swords had betrayed him, and what use was a part of a lawnmower? — There remained only his daggers, compared with the bulk of the Chief Ranger no more than bee stings. But in sheer despera-

tion Bernard seized the one nearest to hand and flung it hard and true at the Chief Ranger's throat.

No more than a bee sting as it was, it made the Chief Ranger bellow. Like most people fond of inflicting pain on others, he himself couldn't bear even a prick without bellowing! — His unmanly roar was his undoing — for who now came running, at the uncouth sound, but the farmer's two big sons!

7

They had been out all night dancing. From the buttonholes of their velvet jackets the big nosegays given them by their best girls hung droopy but still sweet. Their hair was on end, but still glossy with traces of goose-grease. They were so young and strong and jolly — the gay gallivants! — that even after polkas thrice encored, and mazurkas innumerable, they were still ready to tackle any intruder in their mother's dovecote!

"Why, 'tis the Duchess's Chief Ranger!" cried the bigger boy fearlessly. "What be 'ee doing here, Chief Ranger, alarming of our mother's doves?"

"Arresting an escaping criminal," snarled the Chief Ranger, "upon her Grace's orders!"

Both boys stared interestedly up at the ledge. It

was beginning to be light: they could just make out Patience's fair head and slight childish shape.

"Escaping criminal?" repeated the younger incredulously. "Why, her looks just like our little sister!"

14

The End

OF COURSE THEY jolted him off the ladder without the least difficulty: it was from sheer *joie de vivre* that they ducked him in the mill pond. (Bernard added his mite by hurling his last weapon, the part of a lawnmower, in after, and scored a hit on the Chief Ranger's left ear.) As for Tyrant and Torment, the boys just dealt them a good wallop apiece, and left their master to finish the beating when he managed to haul himself out.

How lovely it was for Patience to be given breakfast sitting up in bed (two brown eggs, and four thick slices of brown bread-and-butter) before she sank into sleep under a buttercup-patterned quilt! And how lovelier still, just before she dozed off, to feel her thin little hand clasped in the farmwife's big warm one, and to hear a kindly voice promising she should never have to run anywhere again!

"Truly?" murmured Patience, half-asleep. "Can I truly stay here always?"

"For always and ever," promised the farmwife. "Seeing 'tis just such a little maid as 'ee us have lacked too long . . ."

Exhausted and sleepy as she was, Patience managed to keep awake a moment longer.

"And can Miss Bianca please stay too?"

"If she's that pretty white mouse on your pillow, and if she's been a comfort to 'ee, certainly, my dear," said the farmwife. "We'll fix her up wi' a nice shoe-box, and feed her bacon-rinds every day."

Miss Bianca felt it time to clarify the situation. But she was careful not to hurt the good woman's feelings.

"Personally," she said sweetly, "the idea of a bungalow appeals to me quite enormously. Pray do not imagine me for a moment untouched by so generous and thoughtful an offer! It just so happens —" here she hesitated a moment; and decided not to mention her Porcelain Pagoda — "that I possess a little nook in town already — quite probably spring-cleaned during my absence! Under the escort of the Secretary of the Prisoners' Aid Society (temporarily disguised as a knife-grinder), I shall have no difficulty in regaining it; and you do know how one wants to see nothing's been broken!"

"Indeed I do," agreed the farmwife warmly. "There's no trusting a servant-wench wi' so much as a bran kettle! — But what about the little maid here?" she added. "Will not she grieve for 'ee?"

Miss Bianca sighed.

"No," she said, almost sadly. "Not with two big brothers to play with; not with such kind foster-parents! She may remember me for a little, perhaps, in her dreams — but only in dreams. I would not wish it otherwise," said Miss Bianca gravely, "after all the perils she has undergone. So let me just sing her a last lullaby . . ."

Thus while the farmwife wiped away a sympathetic tear Miss Bianca for the last time sang Patience to sleep. She didn't sing the lullaby about the doves, but a variation composed on the spur of the moment.

Two big brothers and cowslip-balls and violets,

sang Miss Bianca sweetly,

Two big brothers and lambkins in the spring.
One big apron to lay a weary head upon,
A pair of big slippers for a little girl to bring.
Oh cowslip-balls and lullaby, oh lullaby and violets,
Oh lullaby and violets and lambkins in the spring!

As she finished, Patience stirred in her sleep; and put out a hand not towards Miss Bianca, but to the farmwife . . .

"You see?" said Miss Bianca, stepping lightly from the pillow.

"I see you're the cleverest little lady, and the best-hearted, 'twas ever my lot to meet," said the farmwife, "and that lullaby shall ever remain in our family, to be sung God willing to our grandchildren, as a most precious heritage."

2

Bernard and Miss Bianca actually traveled back to the city in the farm gig. It is pleasant to relate that this was chiefly in tribute to Bernard, generally so overlooked; the farmer's sons were so struck by the way he hurled the part of a lawnmower at the Chief Ranger's ear, they insisted on loading his knife-grinder's cart in behind when they drove to market. Bernard felt proud indeed, as he was able to hand Miss Bianca into so swift and commodious a vehicle. They sat together on a nice clean egg.

"Yet even on foot," said Miss Bianca, "and through the forest, at *your* side, my dear Bernard, I should have known no fear! What heroism you have displayed! Your attack upon the Chief Ranger I can compare only with the Charge of the Light Brigade as immortalized by Alfred Lord Tennyson."

Bernard glowed all over. His ears glowed particularly — where he'd almost lopped them off.

"Yet how did you know whither to follow?" asked Miss Bianca. "Did you by any chance — it was a notion of the child's — find my silver chain?"

"It's in my pocket now," said Bernard. "And once I *had* found it, d'you suppose mere bloodhounds would have held me back? — May I keep it, Miss Bianca?" he asked daringly.

She moved a little way down the egg. With every mile that spun behind their wheels she was nearing her Porcelain Pagoda; and the dear familiar company of the Ambassador's son; and all the social duties that so fully occupied her time . . . Fond as she was of Bernard, and much as she admired him, their backgrounds were too different for them ever to be more to each other than they were now. It wasn't that she grudged Bernard the bauble, it was just that to let him keep it would be raising false hopes!

"Dear Bernard, forgive me," said Miss Bianca. "As always, you are my most trusted friend. How many times have I not offered to be a sister to you —"

"Seventeen," said Bernard.

"— and ever with the truest sincerity! But since my chain was a gift from the Boy's mother — and since I'm almost sure there's a dinner party tonight, when of course I shall be expected to wear it — I really must ask you to give it back."

Slowly, reluctantly, Bernard drew Miss Bianca's chain from his pocket. With a peculiarly graceful gesture she bent her neck; as Bernard clasped the clasp, their whiskers, very lightly, brushed.

Then the gig stopped with a jerk. Rough but kindly fingers set down Bernard's cart; scooped up Bernard and Miss Bianca, and set them down too.

"Farewell, farewell!" called the farmer's sons. "And never fear for our new little sister, for her'll be the happiest little maid alive!"

3

The medal struck to commemorate this wonderful adventure caused a good deal of argument. The mice wanted to get the Grand Duchess onto it, and the two bloodhounds, besides the Chief Ranger; this was manifestly impossible, however, and in the end they compromised with the neater if less exciting design of a Ducal coronet shattered, surrounded by mouse-tails intertwiny. Miss Bianca was of course awarded the first, and Bernard the second, and these were in silver. The games mistress (representing the Ladies' Guild) got one in bronze.

The child Patience grew up to be as good and beautiful as she was happy, and married the elder of her foster-parents' sons. They still live all together in the farmhouse in the Happy Valley, and put bacon-rinds out for the mice every night.

THE END